"Can't You Keep Your Mind Off Sex?"

Chase asked.

"*My* mind?" Nicole exploded. "*You're* the one who brings up the subject every two seconds."

"So where are we going to do our...research?" he inquired.

"In the dining room. On the table. That way, there will be enough room to spread out," she informed him.

"I've never done it on a dining room table. Tried a pool table once—" he noted reflectively.

She cut him off. "If you're not talking about studying, I don't want to hear about it."

"How about the living room?" he suggested. "Looks much more comfortable in there. I could start a fire."

I'll bet you could, she thought. "We'd be able to get along just fine if you wouldn't persist in turning everything into a flirtatious encounter."

"I wouldn't flirt with you if you'd stop flirting back," he told her.

"I do no such thing!" she protested, trying to avoid looking into his sexy eyes. It didn't help matters any that the visual messages he was sending her were so tempting...

Dear Reader,

Happy summer reading from all of us at Silhouette Desire! I know you'll enjoy this July's selections as much as I do, starting with a scrumptious *Man of the Month,* Dan Blaylock, hero of Cait London's *Midnight Rider.* This book will send you running to the nearest ranch so you can find a man like this of your very own.

Robin Elliott fans—and there are plenty of you out there—will be thrilled to note that she's made a return to Silhouette Desire with the delightful, suspenseful *Sophie's Attic.* Welcome back, Robin!

And Jackie Merritt, whose heroes are often "back at the ranch," opts for a change of scenery...but no change of excitement...in *Shipwrecked!* Rounding out the month are three books that are simply not to be missed: *Flirting with Trouble* by Cathie Linz, *Princess McGee* by Maura Seger, and *An Unsuitable Man for the Job* by Elizabeth Bevarly. Don't let July go by without reading these books.

So, until next month, go wild with Desire—you'll be glad you did.

Lucia Macro

Senior Editor

CATHIE LINZ

FLIRTING WITH TROUBLE

SILHOUETTE *Desire*®

Published by Silhouette Books New York

America's Publisher of Contemporary Romance

SILHOUETTE BOOKS
300 East 42nd St., New York, N.Y. 10017

FLIRTING WITH TROUBLE

ISBN: 0-373-05722-9

First Silhouette Books printing July 1992

All the characters in this book have no existence
outside the imagination of the author and have
no relation whatsoever to anyone bearing the same
name or names. They are not even distantly
inspired by any individual known or unknown
to the author, and all incidents are pure invention.

® and ™: Trademarks used with authorization.
Trademarks indicated with ® are registered
in the United States Patent and Trademark Office,
the Canada Trade Mark Office and in
other countries.

Printed in the U.S.A.

Books by Cathie Linz

Silhouette Desire

Change of Heart #408
A Friend in Need #443
As Good as Gold #484
Adam's Way #519
Smiles #575
Handyman #616
Smooth Sailing #665
Flirting with Trouble #722

CATHIE LINZ

was in her mid-twenties when she left her career in a university law library to become a full-time writer of contemporary romance fiction. Her library background came in handy while researching this book, her twentieth. This Chicago author enjoys hearing from readers and has received fan mail from as far away as Nigeria!

An avid world traveler, Cathie often uses humorous mishaps from her own trips as inspiration for her stories, although she set this one a little closer to home in a town in west suburban Chicago. Wherever she goes, she's always glad to get back home to her two cats, her trusty word processor and her hidden cache of Oreo cookies!

For Lynne Smith
(a.k.a. Paula Christopher and Lynn Michaels)
for being on the same wavelength
as I am
and
for tuning in
to hear the voices.
Thanks.
Time for a cheeseburger!

One

Nicole Larson had never been one to back down from a fight. So, while hurriedly climbing the steps to Oak Heights Village Hall on this glorious spring morning, Nicole was actually looking forward to confronting the lion in its den. She'd been arguing with Village Hall for months now, trying to get a new position approved for another librarian at the public library. The optimist in her saw this latest summons as a good sign.

"Ah, there you are, Nicole," Police Chief Straud said as she entered the building. "I've been waiting for you."

Nicole smiled at the police chief she'd known all her life. "It's nice to see you, but I can't talk now. I'm on my way for a meeting with the mayor..."

"Actually your meeting is with me," the chief inserted.

"Since when have you been involved in budgeting battles?" Nicole inquired, before adding dryly, "Trust me, I won't get violent in my demands. I don't think police protection for either myself or the mayor will be necessary."

Police Chief Straud grinned. "Now there's a picture. Me protecting the mayor from the feisty town librarian. But seriously, you've been called here for another reason. This isn't about budgeting problems."

"Is something wrong?" she anxiously inquired.

"Now don't get upset," he reassured her. "It's just a project I need to discuss with you. Let's go into my office, shall we?"

Since the village of Oak Heights wasn't large enough to have a separate police building, the police force worked out of the Village Hall municipal building. The force was cramped for space, and rumor had it they were lobbying for new headquarters in a new location. Nicole wondered if that was what the chief wanted to talk to her about—the fact that the police department and the library were both vying for money from a limited budget.

"Chief, I've got those papers you wanted," a fresh-faced police officer said as they neared the chief's office.

"You go on ahead," the chief told Nicole. "I need to look these papers over. It will only take me a minute. You can make yourself comfortable in my office and I'll be right with you."

Nicole entered the chief's office, only to stop in her tracks a second later. The office was not empty. One of the two visitor's chairs was already occupied—by a disreputable-looking ruffian in black leather!

"I'm sorry. I didn't realize there was anyone in here," Nicole automatically apologized, afraid she might have walked in on some kind of interrogation. The man was alone, however. He sat slouched in his seat, pinning her with his dark gaze. There was a definite aura of danger about him.

And magnetism. Unadulterated male magnetism. Raw and untamed. It positively radiated from him, entangling her even though she was clear across the room.

His jeans were well-worn, molding his long legs like a second skin—a soft denim skin that had several jagged holes in it, at the knee and higher up on his thigh. His black T-shirt appeared to be clean, but he looked like he could use a shave. The rolled-up red bandanna across his forehead may have held his somewhat shaggy dark hair away from his face, but it only added to the defiant raggedness of his appearance. He wasn't handcuffed, although he looked like he should be. This was definitely no run-of-the-mill civil service worker.

"Um, I'll just wait outside," Nicole prudently decided.

"Something wrong with my company?" the man drawled in a deep voice.

"There's obviously been some kind of mistake," Nicole began.

"You can say that again," he muttered. "I can't believe they got me."

A prisoner. That's what he was. Handcuffed or not. While the open door was only inches behind her and the man not within arm's reach, Nicole wasn't real eager to stay. Confronting the mayor was one thing, confrontations with criminals simply weren't on her agenda for today.

Some of Nicole's feelings of misgiving and disapproval must have shown on her face because the man's eyes suddenly narrowed. Then he smiled at her. There was a curl to his lips that she found very disconcerting. Criminal or not, the man had a very sexy mouth!

"So, what did they get *you* for?" he inquired mockingly.

"Nothing," she denied indignantly. "I'm not a criminal!"

"That's what they all say."

"Listen, I'm not the one in trouble here. You are."

"You got that right. And I'm about to receive my punishment," he muttered as Chief Straud entered.

"I see you've already met Detective Ellis," the chief said as he rounded his desk.

"Detective?" Nicole heard herself repeating stupidly.

"That's right," the disreputable ruffian confirmed. "Detective Chase Ellis."

Nicole barely prevented herself from openly staring at him in disbelief. Since when had suburban police detectives started looking like this?

Nicole made a conscious effort to look beyond the surface trappings of his appearance for some sign of the discipline, experience and responsibility that surely went hand in hand with his position. If there was any indication of those characteristics, she was hard put to find it beneath the mocking amusement in his brown eyes. Her first impressions were still the strongest. This man was dangerous—to her peace of mind if nothing else! His outrageous behavior so far had already proved that point.

Chase felt no regrets at having led the librarian on. He didn't want to be on this case in the first place. A library was no place for an undercover cop. It was ridiculous, it was downright humiliating. Which, Chase knew, was exactly why his captain had volunteered him for this assignment.

It was no secret to Chase that his captain—a stickler for procedures and paperwork—was irritated with him at the moment, not only for what the captain claimed was Chase's "cavalier disregard for paperwork and following procedural rules" but also for Chase's supposed flirtation with the captain's daughter.

The temporary transfer clear out to this sleepy 'burb on the outer fringes of Chicago's metropolitan sprawl was the captain's way of letting his disapproval be known, not to mention also getting Chase away from the captain's susceptible daughter. So Chase ended up here in Oak Heights, working in another township, assigned to this case—forced to go undercover in a library, of all places.

The librarian looked good, though, Chase decided as she sat down beside him. She had great legs. Chase liked that in a woman.

Her blond hair swished over her cheek before she impatiently tucked it behind one perfectly shaped ear, thus giving him a great silhouetted view of the creamy curve of her high cheekbone and her pert little nose. He already knew from the startled looks she'd given him earlier that her eyes were green. He'd expected them to be blue.

Surreptitiously keeping his own eyes on her, Chase listened as Chief Straud told Nicole about the case. When she'd seated herself, her skirt had ridden up an inch or two, and he watched in amusement as her slender fingers attempted to tug the material back into place.

Aware of his gaze, Nicole shot him a fiery look. The man had his nerve! He wasn't simply eyeing her, he was visually undressing her. What's more, she could *feel* him doing it. Her skin tingled as if he'd actually touched her with his hands instead of just his eyes.

His provocative perusal meandered upward until he eventually met her indignant stare head-on. No words were spoken, but Nicole let him know in no uncertain terms what she thought of his improper behavior.

Chase merely shrugged, his grin communicating his lack of contrition.

"What it boils down to," Chief Straud was saying, "is that we have reason to suspect that the Oak Heights Public Library is being used as a drop-off point for the transfer of communications and monetary transactions by a gambling ring. That being the case, it's been decided that Detective Ellis here will go undercover to investigate this matter further and nail the people involved."

"Undercover in what way?" Nicole inquired. She supposed, dressed as he was, that the detective would make a good derelict. They didn't get that many at the library, but after all, it was a warm place on a cold day for people who had nowhere else to go.

"Undercover as that librarian you've been asking for," Chief Straud explained.

"A librarian!" Nicole couldn't have been more surprised had the chief said Detective Ellis would be impersonating a nun. "It won't work."

"Why not?" Chase demanded. *His* not wanting to do the job was one thing, but *her* not wanting him to do it was something else entirely.

"Because no one would believe it for a minute," Nicole stated.

"Why don't you let me worry about that," Chase returned in what Nicole considered to be a patronizing way. "You just do your bit."

Noticing the rising tension in the room, Chief Straud hurriedly interceded. "All you have to do, Nicole, is go back to the library and say that the village has finally approved the position for another librarian that you've been requesting for so long, but that the position has to be filled right away or funding will be lost. Interview others for the position, aside from Detective Ellis, to make it more realistic—I'm sure you must have some résumés on file—but hire *him* for the job. Don't worry. Should anyone bother checking, we've created a paper trail to cover everything I'm telling you, including an outstanding résumé and background for Detective Ellis. Take a look."

Chief Straud handed Nicole a copy of the résumé, which listed the detective as Alvin Hoffstedder, age thirty-four.

"Alvin?" Nicole inquired.

Chase just shrugged.

"I assume you're not going to show up for your interview dressed the way you are today," Nicole said.

"Oh, I'll be dressed appropriately, don't you worry," Chase assured her wryly.

Chase, also known as Alvin, clearly had a different opinion of *appropriately* than Nicole had. That much was immediately apparent to her the moment he walked in for his interview. Chase/Alvin had left his black leather biker look behind. Instead he was wearing little wire-rimmed glasses, a ridiculous bow tie, and a white shirt. As if that weren't bad enough, his pants weren't quite the right size, being just a bit high in the waist and just a tad short in the leg.

Nicole was really irritated now. In her opinion, Chase's "costume" was a deliberate insult to the profession. Clearly he considered librarians to be a bunch of nerds and had dressed accordingly.

Glancing over at Frieda, one of two circulation assistants on duty that morning, Nicole saw her roll her eyes expressively.

"You must be Alvin Hoffstedder," Nicole greeted Chase. "If you'll just come on into my office, we'll begin the interview."

Closing the door, she didn't even wait for him to sit down before speaking her mind. "Don't you think you're overdoing it just a bit? I thought you wanted to fit in..."

The dangerous coldness of Chase's eyes froze the rest of Nicole's words on her tongue. Leaning close, he brusquely ordered, "Not here." Although spoken at a whisper, the command was indisputably authoritative nonetheless. The sweep of his gaze let her know that he did not consider her office a safe place in which to speak.

A second later Chase stepped away from her, slipping right back into the role of Alvin so quickly that Nicole blinked, wondering if she'd imagined that moment of impending danger. But after a closer look on her part, she could discern a lingering simmer of emotion beneath the bland expression he'd deliberately adopted.

Perturbed, Nicole realized that she had a complicated man on her hands here and she was definitely *not* overjoyed at the prospect of having to deal with him.

Two

"Are you ready to start?" Chase inquired with a blandness that didn't fool Nicole for one minute.

He was still angry with her, she could sense that. Well, the feeling's mutual, she thought to herself in irritation. He hadn't exactly endeared himself to her, either.

Nicole hadn't forgotten the way Chase had deliberately misled her in Chief Straud's office the other day, letting her think he was a criminal. She didn't appreciate being the object of his warped sense of humor. He obviously got his jollies by making others look ridiculous. Not a real good character trait in her book.

"Ready to start what?" she asked, anticipating any number of possible answers, given his track record.

"Our interview," Chase replied with a wicked grin—a new tool in his arsenal of diversionary techniques.

Nicole figured she was as ready as she was ever going to be. Actually, she hadn't anticipated having to interview him.

He already had the job. There was nothing she could do about that. But she supposed it did make sense to go through the motions. It would make his cover more believable—despite the garish bow tie. "Do sit down, Mr. Hoffmeister."

"Hoffstedder," he corrected her. "Alvin Hoffstedder."

"Of course." She'd known that. She just wanted to irk him one-tenth as much as he'd irked her. "So... why don't you tell me a little about yourself?"

"What would you like to know?" he countered.

Why you're looking at me that way, for one thing, Nicole thought to herself. And why you seem determined to make my life difficult. And how soon will you be gone, so that my life can return to normal once more. Aloud Nicole said, "Why don't you start by telling me about your experience in this field?"

"I'm *very* experienced," Chase replied.

His words were accompanied by a look. And what a look it was. More like a caress. His eyes boldly wandered over her, visually stroking her with blatant appreciation. The wire-rimmed glasses he wore didn't diminish the effect of his heated gaze one bit. "If you just check my résumé, you'll see that I haven't had any complaints so far," he murmured softly.

Nicole was momentarily speechless. Damn. He was good at this. The width of her crowded desk was between them, yet he'd still managed to make her breath catch.

Her eyes narrowed. He was doing it on purpose, of course. Another diversion. He was probably laughing up his sleeve at how easily flustered the librarian was.

Her resolve returned tenfold. She would remain calm if it killed her. She'd focus her attention on his bow tie. No man could maintain his sexy machismo wearing a bow tie like that. It was brown with yellow spots and leaned slightly to the left.

There, she congratulated herself as her heartbeat and breathing returned to normal. That hadn't been so difficult.

"Why do you think you're the best candidate for this opening?" Nicole inquired, addressing her question to his bow tie.

"Because I'm good at what I do."

He certainly was, she silently agreed. But bothering her wasn't one of the job requirements!

"What got you interested in this line of work?" she asked.

"The women," he promptly replied.

Nicole almost choked.

"I thought library school would be a wonderful place to meet women," Chase continued. "And it was. Of course, once I got there I became devoted to my work."

I'll bet, Nicole thought to herself. She knew what he was devoted to. Driving her nuts. And apparently chasing anything in a skirt. Great.

Sighing, Nicole returned to her list of questions. "What would you say is your biggest strength?"

"My *biggest* strength?"

The provocative look he gave her made her blush. He'd communicated his thoughts with resounding clarity. What's more, he had the nerve to act as if she were the one bringing sex into the conversation and not him.

Nicole refused to let him get the best of her. She couldn't control the flush on her cheeks, she'd been cursed with thin skin at birth. But she could outstare him. After all, she'd grown up with two brothers, two sisters, and four cats. Outstaring was something she was good at.

So was Chase. He didn't so much as blink. But his satisfied grin made her eyes narrow again. The man was giving her a headache. She refused to even acknowledge the other evocative body aches he was responsible for arousing.

"Is it that difficult for you to think of one of your strengths?" she inquired sweetly.

He leaned closer. "You really want to know?"

"Only so far as it's relevant to your application for the position of circulation librarian," she returned.

"I'm good with people," he announced, leaning back in his chair once more. "I'd say that's my greatest strength."

Good with people? she noted with disbelief. Give me a break!

"And your weakness?" she continued.

Chase was the first to admit that he had a weakness for curvaceous blondes, but he resisted stating that fact out loud. Tempting as it was to aggravate her even further, he wasn't about to say anything to jeopardize the case. He had to admit that he was enjoying himself far more than he thought he would, however.

Teasing the librarian was proving to be an enjoyable pastime. If he had to be stuck in this dusty place he might as well make the most of it. Watching her eyes light up with anger—and awareness, he'd seen that, as well—was just too tempting an opportunity to pass up.

Besides, she looked damn good all riled up. Made him wonder what she'd look like after being made love to for a few hours. That would take the stiffness out of her. The direction of his thoughts put the stiffness *into* him.

Chase frowned and shifted slightly. Teasing the librarian was one thing, getting turned on by her was something else again. He was supposed to be the one aggravating her, not the other way around.

His bookish appearance had definitely seemed to aggravate her. Let me see, Chase pondered. How would a nerdy librarian answer a question about weaknesses?

"My weaknesses?" he repeated. "They're too many to enumerate," he said with a humble meekness that would have made his high school drama teacher proud. Chase thought it was pretty good himself. "I merely try and do my best. I really want this job." Those last words stuck in his throat, but the livid look on Nicole's face gave him the incentive to continue. "And I'll do my best to make you happy."

Make me crazy, more likely, Nicole decided, knowing full well that he was playing up his Alvin routine to the hilt. Why me? she thought to herself. Why this library? Why this cop?

"Thank you for coming," she said politely. "I'll be making my final decision tomorrow and I'll let you know."

"Can't you give me a hint on how I did?" he inquired.

The false anxiety in his voice made her want to kick him. Nicole was certain that the word anxiety wasn't even *in* Chase Ellis's vocabulary. Double entendres, inflammatory statements—those were more up his alley. Besides, they both knew she had no choice but to give him the job, much as she would have preferred telling him never to darken her door again.

"Let's just say that you made quite an impression," she said.

"Then I've accomplished what I set out to do," he had the nerve to admit.

He left quickly, making Nicole think that perhaps he'd correctly read her desire for blood. *His.* It gave her some satisfaction to think that she'd sped him on his way, but deep down she knew that his reasons for leaving were his own.

Nicole was muttering under her breath and reaching for a bottle of aspirin from her desk drawer when Frieda walked in.

"He was an interesting applicant," Frieda noted, handing Nicole three phone messages.

"That's one way of putting it," Nicole returned.

"I've never met anyone named Alvin before," Frieda admitted. "If he gets the job, it might take some getting used to."

"It would?" Nicole knew why it would take an adjustment on her part, the man was obviously intent on driving her nuts. But she wasn't aware of any reason why Frieda would have a problem.

Nicole liked Frieda, had done since the older woman had applied for the job of circulation assistant three years ago. Few employers had been interested in hiring a woman in her late fifties, Frieda had confessed at the time. Her husband was retired and she needed an outside interest to keep her sane, not to mention the additional income. Nicole didn't want her feeling uncomfortable. "Why would it take some getting used to if Mr. Hoffstedder were to get the job?"

"It's his name," Frieda explained. "Alvin. I hear it and my mind thinks—Alvin and the Chipmunks." Seeing Nicole's blank look, Frieda elaborated. "You know, the Christmas songs by those cartoon characters with the high-pitched voices. They're my grandchildren's favorite holiday songs."

"I wouldn't worry about it too much."

"I wouldn't want to make him feel uncomfortable," the kind-hearted Frieda noted.

"Impossible to do!" Nicole declared. She didn't realize how vehemently she'd stated her opinion until she caught Frieda's curious look.

Nicole might know that Chase, alias Alvin, had the skin of a rhinoceros, but no one else in the library did. After all, he *looked* like the mild-mannered kind who'd jump at their own shadow. Nicole hastily rephrased her comment. "I mean, you'd never make anyone feel uncomfortable, Frieda. You're much too empathetic a person to ever do that. I'm sure you're worrying over nothing," Nicole assured her as she accompanied the other woman out of the office toward the circulation desk.

"You mean because he probably won't be getting the position?" Frieda asked.

Nicole was grateful that they were interrupted by Anna Delgado, the children's librarian, but that was before she heard what Anna had to say.

"It's librarians like that last one that give the profession a bad name," Anna announced with a grin. A live wire with seemingly boundless energy, Anna was the resident clown, always ready with a fast comment and a grin. With her wavy dark hair and flashing eyes, Anna possessed an ageless enthusiasm that made people think she was younger than her forty-four years. "Did you see the bow tie on that guy? Someone needs to take him in hand."

If you only knew what lies beneath that mild-mannered exterior, you'd be surprised, Nicole noted. Talk about a wolf in sheep's clothing!

Frankly, Nicole had been somewhat startled at the degree to which Chase had managed to change his appearance. He hadn't done anything really drastic, used a wig or even added a mustache. He'd changed his hairstyle, parting it way on the side and slicking it back. And he'd added the glasses. But his entire physical presence had changed—from the way he carried himself to the way he spoke. All his newfound mannerisms reflected a tentative mild-mannered bookworm.

But when Nicole had complained about his appearance, the real Chase had flashed out for an instant and the fire had been there before he'd covered it up again.

"The important thing is that he has excellent credentials," Nicole pointed out. Falsified, true, she added to herself. But excellent nonetheless. Chief Straud had concocted an impressive cover.

Her temples throbbed even harder. The aspirin wasn't working yet. She wasn't cut out for this cloak-and-dagger stuff, Nicole decided. Those kinds of adventurous days were behind her now. If she wasn't careful, her wayward thoughts were going to get her into trouble. True, she'd never been one to back down from a fight, but saying one thing and thinking another called for a self-censorship that had never been her strong point in the past.

Nicole was afraid she might slip up and say something she shouldn't. She'd just have to treat Chase as if he really *were* Alvin Hoffstedder, librarian. That would no doubt be the easiest thing—the safest, too.

By the time Nicole let herself into her house later that evening, she still hadn't shaken the headache. The food she'd grabbed at a take-out on the way home hadn't done the trick. This called for drastic measures. TollHouse chocolate-chip cookies. Homemade. It was the only sure cure.

Chase had made a major impression on her earlier in the day. She needed something equally powerful to dispel the hold he seemed to have on her thoughts. And as far as she was concerned, there was no better distraction than baking.

Twenty minutes later, dressed in jeans and a T-shirt, wearing a thin layer of flour, Nicole felt much better. The house might be rented, but Nicole had gone out of her way to make it into a home. The kitchen was no exception. A pair of floral watercolors adorned the walls while a poster of the rocky Oregon coastline created a window effect over her kitchen sink. Since she didn't own a dishwasher, she appreciated having something scenic to look at while she was doing dishes.

The tiny earphones tucked in her ears amplified the rhythmic sound of Paul Simon's latest release as Nicole jived her way across the kitchen with a cookie sheet full of the drop cookies. Her hips wiggled to the beat as she opened the oven door and deposited the cookie sheet inside. Then she danced her way back to the bowl of dough. On the way, she noticed that the garbage can was full.

Tossing the oven mitt onto the counter, she gathered the garbage bag in one hand and opened the back door with the other. All the while she was humming along with the music, picking up every fifth word or so.

It was dark outside. The bulb on the back patio light needed replacing. She really had to get to that. In the meantime, Nicole left the back door open so that the light streaming out from the kitchen lighted her way the few yards to the trash can.

Nicole had no premonition of danger. One moment she was trying to sing along with Paul Simon, the next moment she was abruptly grabbed from behind. A hand covered her mouth as she was hauled back toward the open kitchen door. The earphones slid down around her neck, intensifying her feeling of being trapped.

Nicole reacted instinctively. Lashing out with her feet, she tried to kick her attacker. Since he was behind her, that didn't work. So she bit the hand muzzling her.

"Ouch! Dammit!" a familiar voice growled in her ear. "Stop it, you idiot!"

Three

___

Nicole barely had time to assimilate the fact that her attacker was none other than Chase before he spun her in his arms and yanked her to him. "It obviously takes more to keep you quiet," he ground out. "Maybe this will do the trick."

Before she could protest, he covered her mouth with his. Afterward, Nicole was able to think of all the things she could have done to stop him. But at that moment she was so stunned by his behavior that she was momentarily paralyzed.

His mouth silenced hers with just enough pressure to drive her lips apart, annihilating all her preconceived ideas of what a kiss should be. Fast heat. Direct seduction. She tasted his impatience, felt the flare of hunger. She was in over her head, drowning.

He had her wrapped so tightly in his arms that not only was *she* flattened against him, so were her breasts! The leather jacket he wore hung open, so the thin layer of clothing separating them did little to protect her feminine curves from his male domination. The warmth of his body burned through the cotton of not only his T-shirt, but also hers—radiating from the tips of her breasts clear down to her curling toes.

Held so close, Nicole was shocked by the intensity of her feelings as she was filled with an erotic heat that reached every disturbingly intimate hollow of her body. Her senses were overloaded with stimulus: the flex of his shoulders beneath her fingertips, the smell of soap and leather, the sound of her heart pounding in her ears, the movement of his denim-clad thighs against hers. There was no time, no opportunity to think.

By the time Chase had finished kissing her, he'd somehow managed to backstep her the rest of the way into her kitchen.

Releasing her, he said, "Something's burning."

Me! Nicole thought to herself. *I'm* burning!

Blinking against the glare of the kitchen light, the haze finally cleared from Nicole's mind. She was standing in the middle of her kitchen with no clear recollection of how she'd gotten there—except for the memory of Chase kissing her while apparently relocating her as if she were nothing more than a pesky obstacle.

Not satisfied with scaring five years off her life, he also had the nerve to walk into her home completely uninvited. Now he was calmly closing the back door as if it were *his* house and not hers.

Furious at the way Chase had just treated her, Nicole socked him, hitting his arm as he nonchalantly ambled past her. It was an instinctive reaction. Since he was wearing a black leather jacket, she doubted she did any damage. She probably should have slapped him, heaven knew she had reason enough.

Instead she grabbed the oven mitt and yanked a blackened batch of cookies from the oven. After seeing the charred ruins, she wished she *had* slapped him.

"I wouldn't if I were you," he warned her, reading the general direction of her thoughts if not the exact intent. Chase recognized murder in a woman's eyes when he saw it. The jab she'd already given him had been harmless enough, but he didn't want her repeating it. "It's illegal to attack an officer of the law."

"It's illegal to attack a defenseless woman!" she shot back.

"I didn't attack you. You attacked me. Look what you did to my hand." He showed her the tooth marks. "I was merely trying to keep you quiet by kissing you."

"Without my permission."

"There wasn't time to ask," he retorted. "You were about to jeopardize the case, so I did what I had to do. I kissed you."

"How noble of you to make the ultimate sacrifice of kissing me in the name of saving the case," she said sarcastically, stung by his attitude.

"I thought so, too. Actually, kissing a librarian wasn't as bad as I thought it would be," Chase noted reflectively.

"You've got your nerve!"

"So I've been told. Many times."

"And I've been told, many times, that I'm a damn good kisser," Nicole retorted, insulted by his comments. "Providing that I'm with someone I *want* to kiss."

"I know. I said you weren't bad."

"I didn't *want* to kiss you, you arrogant..."

"Uh-uh-uh." Chase shook his head. "No name-calling. You wouldn't want me to have to kiss you again to keep you quiet, now would you?"

"I want you out of my house. Now! You've got no right barging in here this way. I've got a good mind to call Chief Straud and get you thrown off the case."

"Be my guest," he invited her as he sat down at her kitchen table. "Of course, then you'd have to explain why you kissed me back. Could get kind of complicated."

The headache Nicole had been fighting earlier had returned. And its cause was Chase Ellis, the man who was calmly making himself at home, taking a handful of cookies from the plate of those she'd baked earlier.

"Besides, if you did get me off the case, you'd never know who's using your library for illegal purposes," he added between bites.

"You think you're the only one who can solve this case?" she demanded, amazed at the conceit of the man.

"Let me put it this way, sweetheart," Chase drawled. "People weren't exactly lining up to get a crack at going undercover as a librarian, know what I mean?"

"Why are you telling me this? I thought we weren't supposed to talk about the case."

"We aren't." He took another handful of cookies. "Not in your office. It's okay to talk here. While you were in the shower earlier, I checked the place for bugs."

"You what!" Nicole exclaimed.

"Calm down. I was only kidding. About checking while you were in the shower, anyway. I inspected the place earlier. You left your back door unlocked when you were gone this afternoon. Bad habit," he chastised her. "Anybody could have walked in."

"Apparently, *anybody* did. That's trespassing."

He ignored her comment. "And you really should get better locks on your doors. A two-year-old could open these."

"If *you* can open them then that must mean that a two-year-old *can* open them!"

"I'm an expert at locks," Chase stated. "I haven't met a lock I couldn't master."

Or a woman.

Chase hadn't actually said the words, but they were clearly there in the way he was appraising her from head to toe—deliberately lingering on the curves in between. He was touching her with his eyes again. She wasn't going to let him get away with it.

"If you're here to talk about the case, talk about it," she said coldly.

"Friendly, aren't you?" he commented as he took off his jacket and hung it over the back of the neighboring chair.

"Not to cavemen who attack me in my own back yard and scare me half to death," she retorted. Just because he'd taken off his jacket, that was no reason for her to stare at him, Nicole silently chastised herself. She wouldn't do it. She wasn't going to pay any attention to the muscular strength of the arms that had held her earlier. So he looked good in a black T-shirt. That didn't make him any less insufferable.

"Is that what I did?" he questioned in that magically expressive deep voice of his. "Scare you half to death?"

"Among other things." Like making my heart go crazy and my bones melt. Symptoms of shock, she told herself. He'd caught her by surprise. That's why she'd reacted the way she had.

Chase showed no signs of remorse for his behavior. "I needed to speak to you and this was the only safe way to do it. I didn't want to take the chance of someone seeing me visiting you. And showing up at your front door as Alvin the Librarian might cause speculation, as well. I figured I needed to fill you in with some more details about this case, so you won't screw up again the way you did earlier in your office. I'll tell you what we're dealing with here and then lay down a few ground rules."

"Number one of which is for you not to barge in on me uninvited," Nicole inserted.

"I would have thought that my not kissing you would have been your number one rule," Chase returned, his smile a devil-may-care dare.

"That's rule number two," she firmly declared.

"There's something you should know about me. I'm only good at obeying one rule at a time."

"Can't concentrate on more than one thing at a time?" she countered sweetly.

"Oh, I wouldn't say that. I thought I managed to concentrate on kissing you and holding you in my arms at the same time, not to mention getting you inside, as well."

No doubt kissing women, holding them in his arms and making them do his bidding was something Chase had had plenty of experience with, Nicole noted darkly. He was a born womanizer. No man learned how to kiss like that without years of experience.

In fact it shouldn't even be legal. There ought to be a law against a man stealing a woman's reason that way—instantly and so completely. Thank goodness it had only been a temporary disorder. Nicole resolved not to let her guard slip again. She'd keep her mind on the case and that was all.

"The gambling ring we're dealing with here takes bets on professional sporting events," Chase was saying. "On everything from horse races at Arlington to the spread on the Bears games. And this ring is using the library as a drop-off location. What's more, we have reason to suspect that someone inside the library knows about these drops and is assisting in having them proceed without a hitch. Apparently a background check, among other things, cleared you of suspicion—that's why you were let in on this operation. But several other staff members have reason to be under suspicion."

"What do you mean, 'have reason to be under suspicion'?" Nicole demanded.

"I can't say more than that."

"I don't appreciate having my privacy invaded with a background check."

"What have you got to be worried about? You passed."

"I'm grateful, I'm sure," she retorted.

"Good," he returned, unfazed by her sarcasm.

"I hate having members of my staff under suspicion. I've worked with these people for several years. I don't like deceiving them this way. The whole thing makes me feel disloyal and deceitful. I want you to know that if I hadn't been directly ordered to do so, I would not have agreed to get involved with this whole thing."

"Then we have something in common. Because if *I* hadn't been directly and forcefully ordered to do so, *I* wouldn't have agreed to get involved with this operation, either. This isn't my idea of a good time," Chase stated. "I'd rather be out there tracking down *real* criminals, instead of these penny-ante guys."

"If this gang is so penny-ante, then why is money being spent on this case instead of a more worthy cause, like the library? We certainly need the additional funding."

"Let's just say that these guys crossed somebody, somebody quite high up. And that somebody wants this ring broken up before it gets any larger and causes even more problems. But first we need the proof to get a conviction and make it stick. That's pretty much it in a nutshell. So, here we both are, neither one of us wanting to be involved..."

"Involved?" Nicole repeated, alarms going off in her head.

"In this case," Chase clarified.

"Right."

"But since we have no choice, we might as well make the best of it," Chase said, propping up one booted foot on the seat of one of her wooden kitchen chairs, looking as if he were settling in for the duration.

"*You* make the best of it." Nicole pointedly pushed his booted foot off the chair seat. "*I'm* staying out of it. And *you're* getting out of my kitchen." She handed him his black jacket. "Good night, Detective Ellis."

"Alvin," he reminded her. "I don't want you making any more slip-ups at the library. While I'm there, I'm Alvin."

"Fine. At the library you're Alvin. Here you're getting in my way, and outstaying a welcome you never actually had in the first place."

"Are you always this angry at men who kiss you?" Chase inquired.

"Only the really annoying ones."

"Are you annoyed with me?" he wondered aloud. "Or with yourself for kissing me back?"

Chase was impressed by the way Nicole's green eyes were both frosty and fiery at the same time.

"Let's get one thing straight, Detective Ellis. I did *not* kiss you back. If I had kissed you back, you'd know it."

"I can hardly wait," Chase murmured.

"You'll wait until it snows in Hades," Nicole declared.

"A fancy way of saying when hell freezes over, huh?"

"You've got it."

"Lucifer better gather up his snow shovel then. Snow's on the way."

"The only one on their way is you. Out my door."

"Now you've got me curious."

"Heaven forbid," she muttered.

"What makes you tick, Lady Librarian?"

Nicole made no reply. She merely opened the back door a little wider with unmistakable impatience.

"Fine. Don't tell me about yourself. I'll find out on my own," Chase said. "It's better that way. More challenging."

"You just concentrate on your job and we'll all be a lot better off," Nicole told him.

"I'm sorry I startled you," Chase surprised her by saying as he ambled by. "But I'm not sorry I kissed you," he added before walking out the door.

Nicole slammed the door with enough force to make the doorknob rattle. "Arrogant, self-centered, impossible, trouble-making...rebel." Her voice trailed off as that one word brought back so many painful memories.

The cocky swagger, the black leather, the devil in his eyes, the love of a challenge. Nicole had run across that dangerously seductive combination before. She'd been attracted before. And she'd ended up loving the man passionately, wholeheartedly, holding nothing back.

She'd embraced life with the same kind of reckless abandon as Johnny had. It had ended up getting him killed.

Nicole sat down at the table and lowered her head in her hands. Once recalled, there was no stopping the tragic memories as they tumbled forth. She could see it all again, like a horror movie that wouldn't stop playing.

The sun was shining. Johnny had been showing off on his motorcycle, not wearing a helmet—they'd never worn helmets—they'd been invincible in those days...those far away yet almost touchable college days.

The flash of his grin, the thumbs-up sign he'd given her, the glint of the sun on his rakishly long dark hair. She could remember it all, no matter how many times she wished she'd forget—prayed she'd forget.

She heard the throaty rev of the Harley's engine. Nicole squeezed her eyes shut, but it made no difference. The images were as strong as ever. She saw herself standing there watching him. Saw the bike sliding out of control. The turn was too tight. Metal crunching. Her world dissolving. Johnny crashing.

Her fault. He'd been showing off for her. She hadn't asked him to, but she hadn't tried to stop him—and he'd died in front of her very eyes.

With Johnny's death, something had died in Nicole, as well. Recklessness had been replaced with extreme caution. Her passion had been rechanneled into safer areas, like books.

There was nothing safe about Chase Ellis. Aside from the fact that he was a cop, a dangerous profession if ever there was one, he possessed the same kind of reckless defiance that Johnny had. He was the kind of man who went looking for trouble...and always found it. And he was the kind of man who made you yearn for trouble, too.

Nicole saw it now. There were a lot of similarities. Too many. All the more reason for her to keep her distance from the dangerous detective.

Four

Deciding to stay away from Chase was all very well and good. But it was a little hard for her to do when she found herself practically falling over him every two minutes of her working day. Or so it seemed to a beleaguered Nicole.

Chase had only been working at the library for two days now and already she was going crazy. She'd never realized how small the Oak Heights library was until *he'd* come to work there. Since then, the building had simply shrunk. There was no other explanation for it.

Sitting on a park bench, enjoying a brief respite from the library and his company, Nicole dug her spoon into her yogurt carton. Lilac Park was right across the street from the library and she'd taken to eating her lunch out here to get away from the mayhem inside the library. Or was the mayhem inside her?

Nicole sighed. It was a lovely spring day. She should be enjoying the sweet scent of the blossoming lilacs, the cheerful sound of a robin's song. Instead she was brooding about Chase. Or was it Alvin?

She hadn't seen the black-leathered Chase since two nights ago when he'd kissed her. Alvin, however, had shown up for work bright and early yesterday morning. An hour before the library officially opened, Nicole had given Alvin an orientation tour of the building.

It had been an unusual experience. For although he'd been dressed as Alvin—complete with bow tie—flashes of Chase had come through. She remembered one incident in particular.

She'd been explaining the building's L-shaped layout. "This section of the library, where the collection is shelved, is known as the library stacks, or just the stacks."

She'd felt Chase's eyes on the curve of her breasts. He was clearly examining *her* layout, not the building's. And what sexual images he was conjuring up from the word *stack,* she could only imagine. His wicked grin and the direction of his stare gave her a pretty good idea, however.

She'd tried briskly ignoring him. It hadn't worked very well. For one thing, his provocative appraisal had made her heart race. Her breathing, too. Which had only aggravated the situation, drawing even further attention to that part of her body that she'd least wanted noticed.

It had been just one of many times that Nicole had longed for a pert size 32A size instead of what was, in her mind, an overly lush size of 36C.

Unsettled as she'd been, she'd employed sarcasm as a shield. "Since you've obviously shown such interest...in the stacks...you'll be pleased to hear that you will most likely be spending a good deal of your time here. We've been needing someone to read the shelves, check the call numbers and make sure that the books are all shelved in proper order. It's a dirty job, but someone's got to do it," she'd informed him.

"I'm definitely the man for the job," he'd assured her. "Anytime you want your…stacks…or your shelves…read, just let me know. I'd be glad to attend to it personally and I can promise you that I'd give the job my utmost attention."

"Just keep your attention on your job, and we'll all be fine!"

Keeping her distance, she'd gone on to show him the periodical section where the magazines and newspapers were kept, the reference room with its Quiet Please notices on the glass doors, the card catalog and the three small study/conference rooms. She'd ended the tour with the junior room, which housed the children's collection.

"If anyone asks a reference question, you're to refer them to me," she'd told him.

"You don't trust me?" he'd inquired with a boyishly hurt expression.

"Not as far as I could throw you," she'd muttered under her breath, mindful of his comments about the library not being a completely safe place in which to speak.

"Now there's an interesting picture," he'd softly muttered right back.

"You may answer directional questions, Alvin." She'd used his name deliberately. "You may answer questions about the location of the rest room, and where certain items in the collection are housed, like the compact discs and the videos that I showed you. And given your experience with computers—" Chief Straud had assured her that that part of his resume wasn't made up "—you may deal with patrons regarding the two computers and attendant software we have for their use. But I think it would be best that I continue to answer any other questions. At least until you settle in and have had a chance to acquaint yourself with our procedures." She'd added that as a cover for his story that he really was a new employee.

"I'm looking forward to...acquainting myself...as quickly as possible," he'd had the nerve to murmur.

But the moment the remainder of the library staff had shown up for work, Chase had immediately become Alvin, effusively noting how delighted he was to have the position.

Nicole knew it was all an act. He aggravated her so much that sometimes she got the urge to grab Alvin by that little bow tie he wore and shake him... until Chase came out.

She frowned. Now where had *that* thought come from? Earlier scenarios had her shaking Alvin/Chase until he begged for mercy or apologized, which ever came first.

It was disconcerting, being the only one who really knew what he was like. The other women on the staff hadn't looked twice at him, other than to shake their heads at his nerdy appearance and attitude. If anything, they'd taken him under their collective wing, giving him helpful bits of advice over the past two days—on everything from how to unjam the copy machine to how to get a date.

Nicole could just imagine how Chase must be laughing up his sleeve at *that* one. As if a man like him would have any trouble at all finding a date—on a second's notice, no less. The man had danger and sex appeal galore. Couldn't the others see that? He might be disguised, but she still felt that force field around him.

Nicole only had to get within three feet of him and her nerve endings began to hum. She'd actually tested it. As long as she remained further away, she was okay. The minute she got too close, she reacted. Her hands got damp, her thoughts distracted, and her body became all warm and achy. It was very disconcerting.

Oak Heights had been a peaceful place until he'd come to town. She'd grown up there. She'd eaten her first hamburger at Stop 'n Chat, seen her first movie at the Tivoli Theater, and gotten her first kiss in this very park.

Everyone else in her family had since moved away. Her parents to Arizona, two brothers and a sister to California, and one sister all the way to Alaska. But Nicole had stayed behind, returning to her hometown after finishing graduate school.

The small town west of Chicago was close enough to the big city to drive in for the day, but far enough away to retain its own small-town character. It had represented stability to Nicole. She was now head of the same library where she'd studied as a child. There was a continuity in that that pleased her.

Now Chase, alias Alvin, was disrupting her stable existence. She didn't like him for it. She could only hope that he'd find the gambling ring in a hurry so that they could all go back to normal. There hadn't been any breakthroughs over the past two days, unfortunately.

"Daydreaming again?" a mocking voice inquired over her shoulder.

Nicole jumped, almost spilling what was left of the carton of yogurt down the front of her favorite pink suit.

"Dammit, don't sneak up on me like that!" she told Chase.

"Is that any way to speak to a mild-mannered librarian like myself?" he chastised her, pushing his glasses further up the bridge of his nose.

Today his bow tie was red. Since his shirt was pink, this wasn't the best color choice, especially not with his slacks being a yellowy beige.

"What are you doing out here?" Nicole demanded.

"Taking my lunch break."

She hurriedly stuck the remains of her lunch into the paper bag. "I'll leave you to it, then."

"You wouldn't be avoiding me, by any chance, would you?"

"Absolutely," she cheerfully confirmed.

"Chicken," he murmured.

Nicole glared at him. "What did you say?"

"Chicken. My sandwich." He held it up for her appraisal. "Want a bite?"

Oh, she wanted to bite, all right. Him! From aggravation! And he knew it. In fact, he was obviously pleased about it.

"I've already had a bite," she returned, reminding him of how she'd bitten his hand when he'd grabbed her outside her back door the other evening. "It wasn't to my liking."

"Could have fooled me."

"That's obviously not very hard to do, is it?" With that parting shot, Nicole left, rather proud of the way she'd had the last word that time. She could tell by his frown that her comment hadn't pleased him. Good. It was about time he had a taste of his own medicine. See how he liked being aggravated for a change.

But by the time she'd returned to her office, Nicole was feeling a bit guilty about her behavior. After all, Chase was working in her library on a professional basis. Just because he acted like an adolescent, that was no reason for her to follow suit.

This wasn't a game. This was a serious situation they were dealing with here. Nicole certainly knew that she'd been eyeing patrons differently since she'd found out about the illegal activities allegedly taking place in the library. She resolved to try to be more professional in her future dealings with Chase.

But judging from her past track record she wasn't sure how long she'd be able to keep that resolution. The man had a way of blowing her good intentions to smithereens. It wasn't something she was proud of. In fact, Nicole found it downright disturbing.

So she distracted herself with work, cataloging a cartful of new books. Cataloging wasn't something most head librarians did themselves, but Nicole had to wear a number of different hats at the Oak Heights library since they were perennially short-handed. She could have pushed harder for another librarian to take over the technical services work, but the truth was that she enjoyed inspecting the new books as they came in.

Besides, there was something very calming about putting books in their proper classification. It gave her a sense of there being some kind of order in the world, which certainly made a nice change from the general chaos present in the rest of her life at the moment—since Chase had come into her life, to be exact.

The sound of her name being spoken disrupted her thoughts. She looked up to see a familiar face.

"So, Nicole, how are things going at my favorite library?"

"We're holding our own, Leo," she replied with a smile.

Leo Shapiro had been coming to the library for as long as Nicole could remember. An electronics buff, he checked out *Popular Mechanics* on a regular basis. He was a dreamer who marched to a slightly different drummer.

Yes, Leo was one of a kind. Despite the general male trend toward longer hair, Leo still sported a crew cut that could have been lifted straight out of the fifties. Nicole had been somewhat amused to note that a few teenage guys were beginning to sport the same look, only they had kept a tuft of hair on top of their head. She'd even seen a few of the more adventurous types with their names razorcut into their crew cuts.

Leo wasn't the adventurous type. A shy man who wore bifocals that were perennially perched on the tip of his nose, Leo was the personification of an absentminded inventor. Nicole was sure that if he'd been born in the time of Thomas Edison, Leo would have excelled. As it was, Leo was struggling along as best he could, writing technical manuals for electronics companies.

Whenever he visited the library, he always stopped by the glass-encased fishbowl that passed as Nicole's office for a little chat.

"I got a card saying you're holding that new Robert Ludlum book for me," Leo told her.

Michelle was at the circulation desk and could have gotten the book for him, but Nicole knew that what Leo really wanted was to talk.

"I've been waiting a long time for this book," Leo continued. "When I signed up, I think there were already fifteen people ahead of me on the reserve list."

"Ludlum is a popular author. Even though we have more than one copy of the book, a lot of people want to read it." Nicole got up from her desk and pulled the book from the shelf behind the circulation desk where reserved material was placed. "Here you go."

"I understand a new librarian joined your staff," Leo said as he handed her his library card, its well-worn state attesting to the fact that it was used a lot.

"That's right. Alvin Hoffstedder. He's at lunch at the moment."

"Too bad. I wanted to meet him. I have to tell you, I'm glad to see a man in the position. I used to wish I'd studied to be a librarian. I certainly spend enough time in here," Leo added with a laugh. "But the need to work on my inventions was stronger."

"How are your inventions going?"

Leo's face lit up, as it did whenever he spoke about his work. "Right now I'm working on one of those Dick Tracy kind of wristwatch communicators. I'd forgotten all about them until I rented the movie. I'm going to make mine lighter and more compact. The secret is in the screen."

For the next ten minutes Leo's explanation got so technical that Nicole only understood one word out of twenty.

"Well, that sounds interesting," she said when Leo finally paused to take a breath. "You be sure and enjoy that Ludlum book now." She hated having to cut him off, but a line was forming behind him of others wanting to check out their books.

"I'll let you know how I like it," Leo promised. "And tell the new librarian I said hello. I'll look forward to meeting him next time."

The only thing Nicole was looking forward to where Chase was concerned was him finishing this case and moving on. Then maybe she'd stop jumping at shadows and watching for hidden meanings in everything her staff said. Until then...

A frazzled-looking Anna materialized at Nicole's side. "People are talking about the newest addition to our staff!" Anna dramatically announced.

Nicole's heart jumped and her mind began racing. Had Chase said or done something to give himself away? Had she? "What do you mean?" Nicole asked, managing to sound calm.

"I just finished Story Hour with the preschool group. They wanted to know if our new librarian was Pee Wee Herman's brother. It was all I could do to keep a straight face, I can tell you."

Nicole was hard put to resist a grin herself.

"But wait, it gets worse," Anna said. "Then little Suzie Schmitz pipes up and says that her mommy told her uncle, who lives with them even though he's not *really* her uncle, that only nerds wear bow ties."

"What did you do?" Nicole asked.

"I proceeded to read them a book about a lion who was a late bloomer, an appropriate choice since it's about being different."

"Did that work?"

"I think so. They still wanted to know what a nerd was, though. I wasn't able to distract them that much," Anna admitted.

"I remember when George was that age," Michelle inserted. Michelle and Frieda rotated duties as circulation assistant. The single parent of a rambunctious son, Michelle had her hands full trying to make ends meet. "Makes me glad he's six. Sometimes."

"Are things going better for him at school?" Nicole asked.

Michelle shook her head. "Not much. His teacher agrees that George is acting up because of his disappointment over not having seen his father for so long. It's times like this that I just want to strangle my ex."

"Is he still behind in his child support payments?" the ever blunt Anna demanded.

Michelle nodded. "He doesn't hold down one job long enough for me to trace him through his social security number."

"He's pond scum," Anna stated.

"Who is?" Chase inquired cheerfully, having just returned from lunch.

"Michelle's ex-husband," Anna replied.

"You ladies doing a little man-bashing?"

"Not that *you'd* have any cause to worry," Anna muttered in an aside only Nicole heard. Chase had no way of knowing it, but Anna tended to get irate whenever she heard the phrase "you ladies." "Ever heard of Pee Wee Herman, Alvin?" Anna inquired.

"I think we should all get back to work," Nicole hastily suggested before returning to the relative sanctuary of her office—where she could laugh in private. Chase as Pee Wee Herman? It was ludicrous! Oh, Anna, if only you knew...

Five

———

"**O**h, no! It's Mr. Query and he looks like he's on the warpath," Michelle murmured later that day.

Nicole, who'd taken a brief break from an afternoon spent compiling the statistics necessary for the library's annual report, looked across the reading room toward the cherry-faced man bearing down on them with the single-minded determination of a guided missile.

"'I wonder what our charming library board member wants this time," Nicole muttered. Besides my head on a platter, she silently added. The prissy grade school principal had never liked her and seemed to delight in making her life difficult. Maybe she was just being paranoid, but as a friend of hers always said, *Just because you're paranoid, that doesn't mean people aren't talking about you behind your back.*

"Ms. Larson." Mr. Query nodded his head toward her the way a dictator might do to an underling. "Is there someplace private where we can talk?"

He said that each time he came. He should know by now that the only bit of private space—other than the rest room—was her small glass-enclosed cubical. "Certainly. Shall we go to my office?"

She had to clear a chair for him to sit on and in doing so almost knocked over a pile of *Kirkus Reviews* and *Booklist* journals, which she used for book selection purposes. With nearly forty-five hundred books being published each month, the field had to be narrowed down considerably. Therefore she had to read various reviews to justify each purchase. It was a time-consuming job.

"Behind in your reading?" Mr. Query said disapprovingly.

"You know how it is," she replied, telling herself that kicking a board member would *not* be politically correct. "A librarian's job is never done."

"I manage to get my work done."

Bully for you, Nicole thought to herself. "Was there something in particular you wanted to speak to me about?"

"Of course. I wouldn't come here just to have an idle conversation."

"Of course not." Her voice held just a hint of mockery.

"I've come about your acquisition policy."

Again? Surely they'd already had this conversation at least a dozen times. This year alone. "What specifically was it about our acquisition policy that you are concerned about?"

"Those romances. And those videos. Next you'll be buying comic books."

Had Nicole had a larger budget, she might well have. Whatever got people reading was fine by her.

"As I've said before," Mr. Query continued, "the library is our last bastion of culture. We shouldn't display that trash. You've even got rock music on CD, for heaven's sake! Is that the purpose of a library? If people want rock music, they can go out and buy it. That's not our purpose. It's just wasting money on each new fad as it comes into fashion."

"Rock and roll has been around for about forty years now, Mr. Query." Four times as long as "Querulous Query" had been on the library board, although there were times—like today—when it felt as if he'd been around for forty years, as well. "A little long for a fad. And the compact discs have been very popular with our patrons."

"What do they know?" he scoffed with a dismissive wave of his hand.

"It is *their* library, supported by *their* tax dollars."

"They don't know what's good for them. How are they ever going to learn to appreciate the finer points of opera, or the beauty of our greatest pieces of literature...of Thomas Hardy, Anton Chekhov?"

Personally, Nicole had never cared for Thomas Hardy or Anton Chekhov herself. Too depressing. Even so, their works were still well represented in the collection. "Everyone has different tastes," she pointed out.

"Some have no taste at all."

"Some don't," Nicole agreed, looking him straight in the eye and wordlessly telling him that *he* was one of those that didn't.

"And there's another thing," Mr. Query added, apparently having missed her subtle slight. "I don't know that I approve of you hiring this new librarian fellow without consulting the board."

"I have complete authority over personnel," Nicole reminded him.

"I never approved of that policy myself," he told her.

Tough potatoes. Aloud, Nicole said, "Well, I'm sure you must be a busy man. I don't want to keep you. Isn't *Live from the Met* on PBS this evening?"

Mr. Query glanced down at his watch. "You're right. I suppose I should be going."

Thank goodness! It was all Nicole could do to restrain herself from getting up and jumping for joy at his departure.

"Who's the weathered prune?" Chase whispered as she watched to make sure that Mr. Query really did leave the building.

"That's one of our illustrious library board members."

"Bummer."

Nicole laughed. She and Chase exchanged a look of amused commiseration. For the first time there was more than sexual chemistry between them. There was a momentary bridge of shared laughter.

The connection left Nicole feeling as if she'd just consumed an entire bottle of wine. As if she were on top of the Ferris wheel, poised there for that momentary phenomenon of being on top of the world. Exhilarated. Intoxicated.

Chase was looking at her in a way that both charmed and frightened her. Because this kind of seduction was harder to fight than the blatantly physical approach he'd taken before. This was insidious, sneaking up on her and catching her unaware.

She couldn't seem to look away. He'd captured her with his gaze, which was a combination of boldness and subtle invitation. It was hypnotically appealing and infinitely harder to ignore than anything he'd tried on her before.

The special moment was interrupted by Anna. "Only one hour until closing time," she announced.

Feeling shaken at how tempted she'd just been—to do all kinds of wonderfully, dangerously wicked things—Nicole took a deep breath and looked away from the sorcery in Chase's eyes.

"I think we're going to survive yet another day!" Anna cheerfully added.

Maybe so, but Nicole wasn't sure how much more of Chase's potent magic she'd be able to survive without falling victim to its spell.

"So how's the new case going?" Chase's police partner, Carlos, asked him later that night. The two men had gotten together at Nick's Tavern, Chase's old stomping ground, which was as far away from Oak Heights as you could get without leaving the county. There was no danger of anyone seeing them. Besides, the lighting was so dim in the place that Chase could barely make out his partner's face, even though he was sitting right across from him.

"The captain's daughter was asking about you," Carlos added.

Chase groaned. Precocious little Randi was one of the reasons he'd been sent out of town on this case. The captain didn't appreciate the way Randi had been eyeing him. And when she'd plastered herself to him at the spring picnic, his boss had not been amused. The protective papa wasn't about to hear a negative word about his spoiled little darling girl, however. It had been the last straw as far as the captain was concerned.

Two days later Chase found himself yanked off the case he'd been working on with Carlos and loaned out on the reciprocal Metropolitan Enforcement Agency's program— a pool comprised of police officers from all over the county who were called upon whenever a township or village needed additional assistance.

"Tell the captain's daughter that I've died," Chase said.

"She'd just pine for you."

Chase groaned. "Tell her I've got an old injury that would prevent me from satisfying her needs."

"Then she'd feel sorry for you."

"Tell her I've fallen for another woman and there's no hope for anyone else."

"You? Actually *falling* for a woman? Get real! She'd never believe that."

"Why not?" Chase was insulted. "It's happened before."

"Yeah, too many times to count."

"Get outta here!" Chase tossed a handful of bar nuts at him. Luckily Nick's Tavern was the kind of place where the floor was already decorated with bar nuts—among other things. "There haven't been that many women."

"Annette, Danette, Eve, Tammy, Opal..."

"Wait a minute. I never heard of Opal."

"You remember . . . the redheaded waitress with the massaging fingers."

"I never dated her! You did."

"Okay, scratch her."

"I'm sure you did more than just scratch her."

"You got a dirty mind, Ellis."

"I know."

"And there's no way that you'd fall for a woman."

"I fell for Nadine." He'd fallen hard. Made a complete idiot of himself. Allowed her to manipulate him with her pouting ways and her demands cleverly wrapped up as concern. She'd used his love for her to hog-tie him, trussing him up as if he were a damn rodeo cow.

Never again. Never again was he going to let his emotions be used against him. Footloose and fancy-free, that was him.

"Nadine..." Carlos repeated. "Is that the rich dame you were engaged to?"

"That's the one." The engagement had ended right before he and Carlos had first become partners.

"You never did tell me what happened."

"She had her well-connected daddy try to pull a few strings to move me out of police work and into something more to her liking. Like politics."

"What did you do?"

"We fought and I ended up *cutting* a few strings—the ones between me and Nadine. She sailed off into the sunset vowing never to get involved with a cop again. She kept her word, too. Married some rich attorney."

"You're better off without her."

"You got that right," Chase declared emphatically.

"So tell me more about this library job," Carlos said. "Must be tough cooped up with a bunch of old biddies all day long."

"You obviously haven't visited a library lately," Chase returned dryly. "They have some very good-looking women in libraries these days."

"No kidding?"

"I'll admit that I had your neanderthal opinion when I first started out, but I've been...pleasantly surprised, shall we say?"

"What's her name?" Carlos demanded.

"Whose name?"

"The librarian who's pleasantly surprised you."

"Did I say anything about any one woman in particular?" Chase countered innocently.

"You're hitting on a couple of woman at once?"

"I never said I was hitting on anyone."

"It's part of your nature. You can't help yourself," Carlos said.

For some reason, his partner's observation irritated Chase. "Oh, so now you're an expert in human behavior?"

"In *your* behavior, yes. We've been partners for what, almost five years now? I figure I know you better than most."

Yeah, Carlos probably did know him better than most. But even Carlos didn't know him completely. He only knew as much as Chase wanted him to know. That was the way Chase liked it.

"So go on," Carlos prompted him. "What's the dame's name?"

"As if I'd tell you, lughead."

"You're right. Names aren't important. Statistics, buddy. Just give me the bare facts."

Chase tossed another handful of bar nuts at him.

"Oh, I get it. You made the whole thing up," Carlos challenged him.

"Right," Chase retorted. "I conjured up this gorgeous blonde with legs that don't stop and a mouth that can do dangerous things to a man's self-control."

"Spoken like a man who knows what her mouth can do," Carlos slyly noted.

"I can't answer that on the grounds that I might incriminate myself."

"I don't believe it! Leave it to you to land in a pile of manure and come up smellin' like roses. Here I'm feeling sorry for you being stuck out in the boonies, holed up in some dusty old library and you're making out with the librarian. Geez, some guys have all the luck!"

"You said it, buddy." Where Nicole Larson was concerned, Chase was feeling particularly lucky indeed. He had no illusions, she'd be a challenge. But then he'd never been a man to walk away from a challenge.

Early the next morning, Nicole stopped by Village Hall before the library opened. She had to buy a village sticker for her car before the deadline. She was hoping to do so without running into Chief Straud. No such luck.

"Hi, there!" Chief Straud greeted her with a huge smile. "I've been thinking about you. Got a minute?"

Since the last time Nicole had gone to his office she'd ended up meeting Chase, she wasn't sure she wanted to repeat the experience—not that she was suspicious or anything. She refused to be suspicious. Cautious was good, though. So her acceptance was conditional. "I suppose I've got a minute. Not much longer than that, though."

"Good." The chief escorted her through the mazelike hallway to his office. "Go on in." He motioned her ahead of him.

Nicole noticed that he carefully closed the door before sitting at his desk. "So," he said in that jovial voice of his, "how are things going?"

"Fine," she said warily, not sure how much she was supposed to say. Chase had her spooked with all his talk about secrecy and safety. But she supposed that if the police chief's office wasn't safe, she didn't know what place was.

"No problems?" the chief asked.

"If you mean regarding the case, you'd have to speak to Chase... I mean, Detective Ellis, about that. He never tells me anything."

"That's for your own protection," the chief assured her.

Nicole had her doubts about that being Chase's main motivation. He just seemed to like to keep her in the dark—period! Not only that, he also liked grabbing her in the dark and kissing the daylights out of her. Irritating man. Sexy man. Dangerous man.

"Nicole?"

She blinked, refocusing on the chief's amused face. "What?"

"I asked how things are going otherwise. I meant from your perspective. Does it seem as if everything is going smoothly?"

Smoothly? With a rough-riding rebel like Chase? Smoothly? Not exactly the description she would have used.

"Is there a problem?" the chief asked as Nicole paused.

Too many of them to go into. Aloud she noted, "You sound worried. Are you expecting trouble?"

"Well, given the sparks that were flying between you and Detective Ellis when the two of you met here in my office, I did worry that the two of you might not be able to work together on this case." The chief looked more than a tad anxious.

The humor in the situation finally got to Nicole. "Afraid we'd kill each other, hmm?"

"Something like that."

"Relax. I promise not to harm your visiting detective." Much as I might be tempted to, she silently tacked on.

"So you two have worked out your differences?" the chief asked.

"I wouldn't go that far. Let's say that we've reached an understanding of sorts." She understood that he was going to do everything in his power to irritate her. She wasn't sure what Chase understood—that he wasn't going to get away with it, hopefully.

"I'm glad to hear that," Chief Straud said. "I wouldn't want anything jeopardizing the success of this case. Alvin seems to be settling in without incident, right?"

"So far there hasn't been any speculation that I'm aware of." Other than the sexy speculations that Nicole had been having about Chase since the first time she'd seen him in this very office.

"Good. Detective Ellis is apparently very good at this sort of thing."

"Has he been doing this long?" Nicole couldn't resist asking.

"Over ten years, I believe. He came highly recommended, although I was warned that he could be hard to manage."

You can say that again, Nicole silently agreed. *Very* hard to manage. It should have reassured her that she wasn't the only one to think so. Unfortunately it didn't.

* * *

As a result of her unplanned conversation with the police chief, Nicole was a bit late getting to the library to open up. Chase—dressed as Alvin, of course—was already at the building's back door waiting for her. He was alone.

"Sleep in this morning?" he inquired mockingly. "You're late."

"Not really. Just not as early as I usually am."

"Same thing. What's wrong? Have a hard time sleeping last night?" he added in a husky whisper as he moved closer, closing the gap between them. To the casual observer it would seem as if he were courteously trying to assist her in unlocking the door.

Nicole knew *exactly* what he was trying to do! And courteous assistance had nothing to do with it. He leaned over her right shoulder, his breath ricocheting against her cheek when he spoke. "Were you dreaming about me during the night?"

"No," she shot back. "No nightmares, thank heavens. I slept like a baby all night long."

"I'd like to have seen that," he murmured provocatively.

"You have a thing about back doors, don't you?" she muttered as she finally got the stupid lock open.

"Gets you places front doors don't," he replied.

Not with me it doesn't, Nicole vowed. No way. Forget it. The man was entirely too cocky. Too everything. He needed taking down a peg or two and she was just the woman for the job. If she hadn't had more important things to do, that is.

She wasn't going to go out of her way for him. Engaging her in all the thrusts—verbal and otherwise—of a battle of the sexes was precisely what Chase was hoping for. No, the best thing she could do was maintain her distance. She knew that. Now she just had to follow through on it.

* * *

Several hours later Nicole was in the stacks, answering a complicated reference question about Belgian emigrants of the early 1900s, when Chase approached her with something close to desperation in his eyes. Wondering if there had been a serious development with the case, Nicole excused herself and hurried to his side.

"What is it?" she whispered. "What's wrong?"

"See that woman standing over there by the circulation desk? The one with the blue rinse job?"

"Yes." It was Mrs. McGillicutty. She came to the library at least three times a week.

"She just gave me this." Chase surreptitiously held out the note. On it was written, in a floral script, "Where are the sex education books?"

Despite her newfound resolutions to be professional and maintain distance, this was one opportunity Nicole simply couldn't resist. "I know I told you to let me answer the reference questions, but I'm already busy with a patron. I think you can handle this one on your own. Just look in the card catalog under sex education."

"You don't understand," he said. "She wants a book on *sex education.*"

"Yes, I know. You have a problem with that, Alvin?"

"The woman's old enough to be my grandmother."

"So?"

"So, what's she doing asking for a book like that?"

"None of your business," Nicole retorted. "What people check out is their business."

When he frowned, she verbally prodded him. "The card catalog, Alvin. All you have to do is look things up alphabetically. You *do* know your alphabet, don't you, Alvin?"

Chase knew one thing—that he was going to get even with Nicole for this one.

* * *

As it turned out, things got even worse than Chase could have anticipated. "My granddaughter is getting married next month and I just want to make sure she knows more than I did when I got married," the suddenly chatty older woman informed him. "Why, when I was in school we thought babies were born out of a woman's breast. Can you imagine that?"

Chase had no idea why she was telling *him* all this. The collar of his already tight shirt felt as though it was growing even tighter, as was his bow tie, which seemed to be strangling him. This was ridiculous, Chase told himself. He'd dealt with prostitutes in the course of his police work and never batted an eye. Hell, he'd even gone undercover as a pimp on more than one occasion.

But there was just something about *this* woman talking about the subject of sex that disconcerted him. She really *did* remind him of his grandmother.

Things didn't improve when the woman actually had the gall to pat him on the cheek as if he were a nine-year-old. "You're a nice young man," she declared. "I thought I'd be embarrassed speaking to a male librarian, but you've made me feel much better. Are you married?"

"No."

"I still have two granddaughters who are single..."

"I have to take care of my aging mother," Chase quickly fabricated. "I spend all my spare time looking after her."

"Too bad. Well, if your situation changes, you be sure and let me know. I come to the library a lot."

Great, Chase thought to himself. Not only was this case going nowhere fast, but now he had a matchmaking grandmother hot on his trail.

He checked out the woman's books as quickly as he could. The automated circulation system had proved easier for him to master than anything else in this stupid library. Computers he'd dealt with before.

In fact, Chase was hoping that the library's computerized circulation records might supply him with some clues, allow him to see a pattern. One should never overestimate the intelligence of the criminal mind. It was possible that one of the ring members had been careless and checked out material on their favorite subject: gambling and mathematical probabilities. He'd tried to access those records while no one was looking, but had had no luck. An access code was probably required. He'd have to ask Nicole for it.

It was just one of several things he needed to discuss with the lady librarian. Not the least of which was the way she'd put him on the spot just now—*The G-spot* to be exact, one of the books the grandmotherly type had just checked out.

Yep, Chase noted while admiring the sexy sway of Nicole's walk as she crossed the reading room to help another patron. He and Nicole definitely had a few things to settle—including that little quip about Pee Wee Herman.

Since Chase had actually used that character as a model for his role as Alvin, he supposed he shouldn't be insulted by the remark. It just meant that he was playing his role well. Not that he'd had any doubts about his ability to do so. After all, how hard could pretending to be a librarian be?

This reference stuff wasn't so difficult. Embarrassed or not, he'd found the books the grandmotherly type had been looking for. He'd gone to college, he knew how to use a library. There was no reason for Nicole to have made such a big deal about him not answering reference questions without her permission. Hell, any idiot could look up something in a cabinetful of cards. His next question wasn't as straightforward, however.

Nicole was still in the stacks when a woman came up to him a few moments later. "I need to know what time the sun sets in San Francisco on September 9," she asked him.

It sounded like a dumb question to Chase. "What do you want to know that for?"

"I'm writing a book set in San Francisco."

"What kind of book?" Chase inquired, stalling for more time.

"A romance."

"Have you checked out the library's romance collection?" He knew where those were, he'd been shown the crowded paperback racks during his orientation tour.

"I don't want a romance at the moment, thank you," the woman said in exasperation. "I'd just like an answer to my question."

"Sure thing." Chase took the woman over to the card catalog and looked under San Francisco. There he found San Francisco—Description; San Francisco—Earthquake and Fire; San Francisco—History; San Francisco—Social Conditions. Nothing about San Francisco—Sunsets.

Okay. First he'd try for the description books, which looked like they were actually guidebooks, then if that failed he'd try one of the books on social conditions. After all, that's when any city's social life began—after sunset. Everyone knew that.

He found a nice thick guidebook on the shelf. "It should be in here somewhere," he murmured hopefully.

It wasn't.

"I didn't think my question was that complicated," the woman complained after they'd looked through several other books on San Francisco. "I just want to know what time the sun sets in San Francisco on a certain day."

"I know, I know," he said impatiently. "Can't you just fudge the answer? Who's going to know the difference? It's not as if you're writing a real book or anything. It's just a romance.''

Having just overheard Chase's comment from the next aisle over, where she was helping another patron, Nicole almost had an apoplexy. Excusing herself from the patron she'd already helped, she hurriedly came to the rescue.

''I'm sorry,'' Nicole apologized with her best public relations smile, ''Mr. Hoffstedder is new at our library. He only started a few days ago and isn't familiar with everything yet.''

''I'm trying to get familiar as quickly as I can,'' Chase had the nerve to say.

''I know you are,'' Nicole retorted with a frosty look. ''You may go back to the front desk now, Alvin. I'll take over from here.''

Nicole led the woman to the *Farmer's Almanac,* where she quickly found the answer for her.

To Chase's surprise, when Nicole returned to the circulation desk, she actually sought him out. ''May I speak to you for a moment, Alvin?''

It was a rhetorical question since she didn't wait for an answer, instead tugging him aside so they weren't within earshot of anyone else.

While amused at her behavior, and pleased to have her hand on his arm, Chase hoped she wasn't going to say something incriminating. He wasn't sure it would be in character for Alvin to quieten her with a kiss the way he had at her house the other night.

Kissing her was definitely on his mind, however. How could it not be when she was leaning so close to him, those luscious lips of hers a mere breath away? He wondered what she was up to.

Despite the standoffish way she'd been acting toward him lately, Chase knew she felt attracted to him. He was attracted to her, too. She had a lot of passion. It was flashing in her green eyes right now as she whispered, "My house. Tonight. Eight o'clock. Be there."

A second later she was gone.

Chase's smile was most un-Alvinlike. Now *this* was getting interesting. Lucifer had better get out that snow shovel, Chase decided, because it looked like Nicole would be kissing him back sooner than even *he* had anticipated!

Six

This time Chase had the decency to quietly tap on the window on her back door instead of just waltzing on in. She was waiting for him.

He was dressed all in black again. Nicole wondered if he knew how roughly dangerous and rugged he looked. She suspected he did. Then she wondered if he knew how fast her heart was beating. She hoped he didn't.

After changing clothes three times, she'd finally decided to wear navy cotton slacks and a crisp red-and-white striped cotton blouse. While Nicole didn't want Chase to think she'd dressed up for him, she also didn't want to look like a slob.

She'd left her hair loose. The honey-colored ends fell into place just above her shoulders with a smooth naturalness that indicated an excellent cut. Now if she could keep her voice as smooth and natural, she'd do just fine.

"Good," Nicole said with intentional briskness. "You came."

"Of course I came." His voice was caressingly intimate. "How could I turn down an invitation like the one you gave me?"

"Don't get your hopes up."

"My hopes aren't the only thing rising," he murmured.

"We're not here to discuss your physical ailments," she shot back with a speed that made Chase grin.

"Too bad," he murmured. "I have the feeling you'd be able to cure a lot of my... ailments."

"If you're not careful, I just might give you a few additional ailments," she warned him darkly. "Like a black eye."

"You know, I had no idea librarians were so bloodthirsty."

"Listen, if this is going to work at all, you're going to have to make some changes... starting right now."

"Sure. I'm open to suggestions. Variations. Just tell me what you want," Chase suggested provocatively.

"I want you to stop behaving like an oversexed adolescent and concentrate on the matter at hand!"

"The matter *of* hands?"

"*At hand!* That's exactly what I'm talking about," Nicole said in exasperation. "You turn everything into a sexual innuendo and I'm tired of it, Detective."

"Okay. You made your point. Got anything good to eat in here?" Chase asked as he opened her refrigerator and peered inside. "I skipped lunch."

She blinked, momentarily surprised at his sudden change of subject, before reacting instinctively. "Get out of there." She automatically pushed the refrigerator door shut.

"You hiding your millions in the crisper bin or something?" he inquired dryly.

"Of course not."

"Then what's the big deal?"

"You can't just walk into someone's house and go poking around in their refrigerator. It isn't polite."

"I never claimed to be polite," Chase pointed out.

"Yes, I had noticed that from the very beginning—when you deliberately let me think you were a criminal that afternoon in Chief Straud's office."

"That should teach you not to jump to conclusions."

"Is that why you did it?" she pressed him. "To teach me a lesson?"

"Look, I'd just come off another undercover operation." Been *pulled* off by his irritated captain was closer to the truth, but Chase saw no point in telling Nicole that. "That's why I was dressed the way I was. I'd been undercover."

Under whose covers? Nicole wondered but didn't say aloud.

"That's no excuse for deliberately trying to make a fool of me," she said. You sound just like a prim librarian, she noted in disgust. Had Chase reduced her to this? The man really was a hazard.

"You made yourself look foolish all by yourself. And you're still being foolish. I see you haven't replaced your locks yet," he noted disapprovingly.

"We're not here to discuss the security system of my house. We're here to work. That's why I invited you over tonight. To give you a crash lesson in reference work."

"Not until I eat," he stated.

"I'm not making you dinner." Nicole resolutely stifled the guilt that making such an inhospitable statement inspired. It was completely against her nature to be so ungracious— she'd been known to feed most of the block given half a chance. But she knew if she gave Chase an inch, he'd take a mile...or two...or three.

"Who asked you to make me dinner? All I need is some bread, mustard, roast beef, tomatoes, lettuce, mayonnaise..." He licked his lips, reminding her of a hungry lion on the prowl. "Some pickles, maybe."

Nicole could see they wouldn't get any work done until she let him eat. Besides, she decided philosophically, it was better that he take a bite out of a sandwich than out of her.

Sighing, she moved away from her defensive position in front of the refrigerator and said in a resigned tone of voice, "I've only got ham, no roast beef."

"I'll make do." In no time at all he'd gathered up his ingredients while Nicole got out some eating utensils for him.

"Wait a minute!" She pulled away the plate she'd been on the verge of handing him. "You claimed you skipped lunch, but I seem to recall you munching on a chicken sandwich at the park."

"That wimpy sandwich doesn't count." Chase took the plate from her and plopped a five-inch-high mega sandwich on it. "Now *this* is a sandwich."

"For ten people, yes."

"I've got a big appetite," he told her with a wicked gleam in his eyes.

"To match your big ego."

"Among other things."

Nicole rolled her eyes. The man was really something else!

"Besides," he added as he sat down at her kitchen table, "I spent most of my lunch hour on a pay phone. And any sandwich you can eat while talking on the phone is definitely a wimpy sandwich. You need two hands for a sandwich like this. Most things worth doing require both hands," he informed her in that tempting voice of his.

"What were you doing on the phone? Calling your girlfriend?" Oh, right, Nicole, she instantly chastised herself. Why not just hand him a reason to accuse you of being jealous? Talk about handing him a loaded gun...

"I did speak to a sultry redhead named Annette," Chase recalled with a slow smile.

"Forget I asked," she retorted, as irritated with herself as she was with him.

"She works down at the lab. I was trying to get some more information about the case."

The case. Good. That was a much safer subject. "Did you learn anything?"

"Sure did. Annette likes spicy food and mud wrestling."

"I meant about the case!"

"I didn't learn anything that you need to worry about."

"It's my library," Nicole reminded him.

"It's the *public's* library," Chase corrected her. "Possessive little thing, aren't you?"

Nicole took umbrage at his comment. "As head librarian, everything that goes on in the library is my responsibility."

"Really? So you're responsible for the gambling bets being placed in the library? And you're also responsible for the two teenagers who make out in the back conference room? If so, I hope you pointed out a few books on birth control and planned parenthood first."

"Are you trying to tell me that the conference room is being used as . . . ?"

"A lover's hideaway," Chase supplied helpfully. "Yep."

"But there's no lock on the door!"

"They didn't seem real concerned about that drawback."

"I'll check into it."

"I don't know," he murmured mockingly. "It might be too much for your delicate eyes. All those entangled legs and arms . . ."

The image was vivid in her mind's eye. Chase's arms around her, her legs entangled with his, their bodies twisting together . . .

"How did we get onto this subject anyway?" Nicole demanded, leaning against the kitchen counter and nonchalantly fanning herself with a recipe card.

"Because you can't keep your mind off sex?" Chase suggested before taking another hearty bite of his sandwich.

"Me?" Nicole protested. "*You're* the one who brings up the subject every two seconds."

"So where are we going to do our...research?" He made it sound as if they would be researching each other.

"In the dining room. On the table. That way there will be enough room to spread out."

"I've never done it on a dining-room table. Tried a pool table once—" Chase noted reflectively.

Nicole cut him off. "If you're not talking about studying, I don't want to hear about it."

"How about the living room?" He leaned to his right to get a better view of the comfy stuffed couch, plush carpeting, and gas fireplace he could see through the open archway leading out of the kitchen. "Looks much more comfortable in there. I could start a fire."

I'll bet you could, Nicole thought to herself. But I'm not letting you get close enough to me for that. The further away he was, the better. The table was huge. It would provide a handy barrier.

The problem was that Chase insisted on sitting next to her instead of across from her the way he was supposed to.

"Are you sure you want to sit there?" she asked him.

"Absolutely."

"You're comfortable there?"

Chase nodded.

"Good." She got up and took the seat across from him. "Then I'll just move over here."

"You move any further away and we'll need walkie-talkies to communicate."

"We'd be able to communicate just fine if you wouldn't persist in turning everything into a flirtatious encounter," she told him.

"Flirtatious encounter? I like the sound of that."

"I don't."

"I wouldn't flirt with you if you'd stop flirting back."

"I do no such thing!" Did she? Nicole worried. Had he picked up on her own awareness of him? What kind of message was she sending out? He hadn't caught her eyeing him, had he?

She watched him cautiously, trying to gauge how much he knew. How much *could* he know? she asked herself. *You* don't know how you feel about him, so how could *he*?

She found no answers in his dark brown eyes. In fact, she'd deliberately avoided looking into those eyes for too long at one time, because the more she looked, the more she liked. His eyes sloped downward at the outer corners, giving him a slumberous sexy look. It didn't help matters any that the visual messages he was sending her were so tempting.

He's just amusing himself with you, she reminded herself. He's just trying to fluster the lady librarian, as he'd called her. She was irritated that he was succeeding. "I'll bet you were a difficult student in school, right?"

"What gives you that idea?" he countered.

"Your stubborn determination to do whatever you damn well want regardless of what you're told."

"Drove my drama teacher nuts, too," Chase admitted cheerfully. Not to mention his police captain, which he didn't.

"You took drama classes when you were in school?"

"I was the best damn Romeo Lincoln High School ever had."

"On the stage or off?" Nicole inquired.

"Cute. Very cute."

His wry smile invited her to smile back. She did.

So he had taken drama courses. That explained why he was able to project so much emotion into his voice. When he was Alvin at the library, his voice was just a bit higher than usual, lending it a slightly wimpish quality that was totally at odds with the true deepness of his expressive voice. And when he lowered it and added that husky touch of temptation, Nicole believed Chase could sell ice cubes to the eskimos.

"My dad was a drama teacher," Chase told her before adding, "You seem surprised."

She was. "This is the first time you've referred to your family."

"Well, I've got one."

Did that mean he was married? He didn't wear a wedding band, but then he *was* undercover. "You have a wife? Kids?"

He looked at her as if she were crazy. "No way! By family, I meant father, mother, sister, grandmother...which reminds me, that was a low-down sneaky trick you pulled on me this afternoon."

Nicole frowned, unable to follow his abrupt change of subject. "What are you talking about?"

"The lady with the blue rinse job..."

"Ah, Mrs. McGillicutty."

"Right. Turns out, she wanted those books for her granddaughter, who's getting married." Seeing Nicole's Cheshire cat smile, Chase immediately got suspicious. "What? What are you smiling at?"

"Mrs. McGillicutty doesn't have any grandchildren."

"Are you sure?"

"Positive."

"Are you saying that she checked out those books for herself?"

"I'm not saying anything. But she does came in once a month and hands whomever is at the desk a note asking for the sex education books."

"You set me up!"

"You deserved it."

"Why? What did I do?"

"Aside from deliberately trying to drive me crazy, you mean?"

Chase nodded. "Aside from that."

His ready agreement made her laugh.

"You don't do that often enough," he told her.

She made the mistake of looking at him. Her laughter stopped and the warm and achy needing feeling started.

Chase said nothing further, but his dark eyes were very expressive as he focused his gaze on her parted lips. He telegraphed visual messages to her. They came in loud and clear. *I want to kiss you. I want my mouth on yours. Just there.*

Licking lips that had suddenly gone dry, Nicole could almost taste him.

That's it. You want it, too, don't you. Feel it...

Startled by the strength of her emotions, Nicole forced herself to look away and break the eye contact before further contact ensued—physical contact!

Taking a deep breath, she had to really concentrate to make sure her voice didn't come out all wobbly and breathless. "Back to business," she stated with passable firmness.

Chase's smile was smug with male satisfaction. "Whatever you say. We were talking about the strange characters who come to your library."

Eager to get onto a safer conversational level, Nicole was more forthcoming than she normally would have been. "Mrs. McGillicutty isn't that strange. We have one man who comes in and checks out every blue book we own."

"Blue book as in...?" Chase didn't want to jump to any conclusions. Too many of them had turned out to be incorrect where Nicole was concerned.

She blushed, furious with herself for having chosen this particular example. "Blue book as in any book that is the color blue."

"That qualifies as being strange, all right. How about gambling?" he smoothly inserted. "Any patrons got a thing about that subject? I'm going to need the access code in order to review the circulation records. See who's checked out books on gambling or mathematical probabilities during the past year."

"There is no code," Nicole replied.

Chase frowned at her. "What are you talking about? I tried to access that information and couldn't get at it."

"That's because the information isn't available."

"Come on. Your circulation records are computerized. There must be a way..."

"No, there isn't. The minute a book is returned, it's erased from the system."

"You can't be serious."

"Oh, but I am. Very serious."

Coming from a department that was computerizing everything at the entry of a license plate number, Chase hadn't expected this kind of a roadblock. "That's ridiculous!"

"No, it's not," she denied, annoyed by his attitude. "It's deliberate. We don't want the privacy of our library patrons intruded upon. And I'm not alone on this matter. It's something we as librarians have had to deal with since the advent of computerized records. Censorship and the right to privacy are important issues and the American Library Association is clear in its position. That kind information could be abused much too easily. So when you clear charge a book..."

"When I zip the book's bar code under the infared light..." Chase translated.

"It's gone." Nicole snapped her fingers.

"What about before that? Before the records are erased?"

"The books aren't listed by title. Or even by number of books checked out."

Chase was aware of the privacy issue regarding records these days. But since he'd never worked in conjunction with a library before, he hadn't tied the privacy issue into something as seemingly innocuous as circulation records. Besides, he was on an official investigation here. "You're deliberately trying to make things difficult, aren't you?"

"We're deliberately trying to protect the rights of those who use the library."

"Even if those people are criminals?"

"You have to realize, Chase, that privacy is a very touchy issue these days."

"I don't want to hear about it." He sounded thoroughly disgusted. "Crime is a touchy issue, too. How do you expect me to solve this case when you tie my hands?"

"The system was set up this way long before you came along, I can assure you."

"Oh, that makes me feel much better," Chase noted sarcastically.

"Just try and imagine the kind of chaos that would occur if everyone had access to that information. You'd have a Big Brother state when your neighbor knows the type of books you read."

"When we check out a patron's books at the desk, *we* know what kind of books they're reading," he reminded her.

"That's bad enough without centralizing that information. Besides, we're not supposed to notice what people check out."

Ah, but human nature being what it was, chances were they did. Chase decided that he'd be better off pumping Michelle and Frieda about the books people had been checking out lately. And pursuing his other options.

"What's that look for?" Nicole demanded suspiciously.

"What look?" he inquired innocently.

"That cat-that-ate-the-cream expression."

"You're imagining things." Chase changed the subject. "Can you at least tell me why Frieda acts so strangely around me? I get the feeling she'd hiding something. She insists on calling me Mr. Hoffstedder and not Alvin."

"Frieda's trying not to hurt your feelings," Nicole told him.

"What are you talking about?"

"You remind her of a chipmunk."

"What?"

"It's the name. Alvin. Seems her grandchildren's favorite holiday songs are by..."

"Alvin and the Chipmunks," he supplied with a grimace.

"Right."

"And that's why she calls me Mr. Hoffstedder?"

"Right again. You're not suspicious of Frieda, are you?" Nicole demanded.

"I"'m suspicious of everyone."

"Including me?"

"You're safe. For the time being."

Before she could ask him what that meant, he went on to say, "Tell me more about this janitor the library has. What's his name? Drayton? Dayton? I never see him."

"His name is Dayton, and you're not supposed to see him. He cleans the library after hours."

"Which would give him the perfect opportunity to plant information in whatever books he wanted to. I want to meet him," Chase declared.

Nicole's protective instincts immediately came to the fore. "Dayton is as sweet a man as you could hope to meet."

"That's irrelevant."

"Look, I know it couldn't be Dayton."

"And how could you know that?"

"It's confidential."

"Want me to have Chief Straud talk to him?"

"I don't want you bullying him! He's easily intimidated."

"Sounds like the type who could be talked into helping this ring out."

Nicole weighed her options. Telling Chase more about Dayton would mean breaking a confidence, but it might also protect Dayton from a traumatic interrogation and possible humiliation. Reluctantly she opted for revealing the man's secret. "Look, Dayton is functionally illiterate. He couldn't be placing anything in specific books because he wouldn't be able to read the titles. I'm trying to convince him to let me tutor him, but he's a proud man..."

"He wouldn't have to read the titles. Maybe they just tell him to place it on the top shelf, third book from the right."

"And each time a book is shelved, that third book from the right could well become the fourth book from the right," Nicole pointed out.

"I still want to meet him."

"Fine. I was going to have him come in a bit early tomorrow night to help shift some books. You can meet him then, and help him move the books, as well. Nothing like working together to sneak past someone's defenses, right?"

"What are you so het up about?"

"I told you. I don't like having suspicions cast on my staff."

"Why not? Because it might make you appear bad for having hired them?"

"Because they're good people."

"Good people can do bad things. Make mistakes. No one's perfect."

"Some people are less perfect than others," Nicole retorted.

"Meaning me, I suppose."

"I still say that this gang could be using the library without anyone on the staff having to be involved."

"We have it from a reliable source that someone inside is involved," Chase said.

"What source?"

"You just stick to your job, and I'll stick to mine. Don't start playing Nancy Drew," Chase warned her.

"How do you know about Nancy Drew?"

"I heard Anna talking about some girl who came in this afternoon and checked out a pile of Nancy Drew books."

"They're very popular," Nicole confirmed. "So are romances." The second she said that, Nicole knew she shouldn't have. "About that source of yours..."

It was too much to expect Chase to pass up an opening like that.

"Forget my source. Let's get back to romances. Read many yourself?" he inquired with more than casual interest.

She decided the best offence was a good defense. "Yes. Have you?"

He looked as if she had accused him of wearing dresses. "No way!"

"I suppose Rambolike violent thrillers are more up your alley. Or do you prefer comic books?"

"I like westerns. Louis L'Amour. Zane Grey. That sort of thing. Not that I get much chance to read at all."

"Reading westerns is no different from reading romances."

"Sure it is. Westerns are real. Romances aren't."

"How do you figure that?"

"The things that happen in a western could well have happened."

"And you don't think that the things that happen in a romance could happen?"

"Happily-ever-afters are only found between the covers of a book."

That told her a lot about his philosophy on life. He clearly didn't believe that long-term commitments between a man and a woman were meant to work out. She should have guessed as much. "All I'm saying is that you should respect other people's choices and give them the freedom to read what they want." Seeing the look on his face, she said, "Forget it. It's hopeless trying to get you to respect anything. What was I thinking of?"

"Me."

"Right," she said in exasperation. "I think about you twenty-four hours a day and wonder how soon you're going to be done with this case and leaving."

"You know, if I were a more sensitive guy I'd be hurt by that last comment."

"You know, if you were a more sensitive guy, I wouldn't have had to make that last comment," Nicole shot back.

"You're a hard woman. Have you always been this unapproachable?"

"No." She hadn't been unapproachable with Johnny. Not at all.

Nicole's eyes clouded at the memory. She'd met him her first day on campus. She'd been an excited and eager freshman. It was her first time away from home, her first shot at independence. Nicole had also taken her first reckless move by walking up to the dangerously good-looking guy on the motorcycle and asking for directions to the campus bookstore.

He'd offered to give her a lift. She'd taken him up on it. No, she'd hadn't been the least bit unapproachable with Johnny.

"There was a time..." she murmured before trailing off.

"Go on," he prompted her.

Nicole shook her head as if to clear it from the lingering thoughts. "Nothing." She felt restless. Jittery. Unable to sit still a moment longer, she jumped to her feet. "How about some coffee?"

"Why do I have the feeling that you stopped just as it was getting good?" Chase noted ruefully. "I hope this isn't a habit of yours."

Nicole noticed the newfound gentleness in Chase's voice and was entranced by it. He was getting too close.

She used words as a defense. "My habits are no concern of yours." Her tone of voice completely lacked conviction, she noted in dismay.

"Aren't they?"

She shook her head and skittishly tried to sidestep her way past him. She didn't get very far before Chase stopped her.

His warm fingers curled around her arm, effectively halting her in her tracks. His touch was temptingly coaxing as he slid his hand down her arm until his fingers were entwined with hers.

Desperate, Nicole used her free hand to slide one of the heavy volumes on the table toward him. "This book covers a lot of the basics of research. I suggest you take it home and read it."

I'd rather take you home. She waited for Chase to say the flirtatious words. He didn't. Instead he slowly but surely drew her closer.

Her heart stopped. She knew what he was doing, what he was going to do. He was going to kiss her. This time she had a chance to voice a protest. If she could only get her brain to function, and her lips to do more than part.

She couldn't. She didn't. His lips touched hers and she was lost.

Curiosity had gotten her into trouble before. It did again. She wanted to know...had it just been surprise last time, or had it been Chase? Would her blood catch fire the same way it had before...even though she'd known he was going to kiss her?

She soon got her answer. Yes. Oh, most assuredly yes! It was even better than before. Just as explosive. Just as hazardous. But even more powerfully irresistible.

When Chase tugged her down onto his lap, she could feel the primitive needs unfurling deep within her. She could also feel *his* need, the unmistakable strength of his arousal. Logical thought went out the window. Sliding her arms around his neck and leaning closer, Nicole allowed herself the momentary luxury of melting in his arms.

Chase could taste her response in the pliable warmth of her lips. She was all fire and passion. Somewhat dazed, he recalled her promise that when she wanted to kiss a man, he'd know it. She was absolutely right. Chase *knew* she wanted to kiss him. And that knowledge was incredibly arousing.

Like a magical storyteller weaving his fantasies around her, Chase captured her not with force but with persuasion and passion. Drawing her in, he immersed her in the pleasure. Then he embellished on that theme by increasing the intimacy of their kiss, his tongue subtly moving forward to savor the dark recesses of her mouth.

Nicole became an equal partner in the sorcery. Her fingers were kneading into his shoulder with catlike pleasure as she returned his kiss with abandon. She invited, he accepted. His tongue engaged hers in a heated exchange, gliding together and tangling, stroking. He tempted, she yielded.

Chase wasn't content to merely seduce her with his kisses. He excited her with his touch. His fingers moved in an erotically slow progression from the nape of her neck to the small of her back. Tugging her shirt from the waistband of her jeans, Chase slid his hands over her bare skin, murmuring his approval. The tantalizing drift of his caress left her breathless.

Nicole shivered with delight as his lips left hers to explore new territory—the curve of her cheek, the tip of her earlobe, the delicacy of her throat.

One moment she was floating, sheltered from reality…and the next she was holding on for dear life as Chase almost dumped her on the floor!

"Wha-aat?" Nicole managed to regain her footing as Chase released her to grab his right arm. "Are you all right? What happened?"

Chase looked completely disgusted with himself. Frustration and self-conscious derision were written all over his scowling face. "I cracked my elbow on the edge of the table. My funny bone." His smile was grim. "My arm's numb. Just give me a second and it will be better."

To Nicole it was a sign from above, a signal from some kind of guardian angel looking after her. Released from the intoxicating spell he'd cast over her, she knew exactly what she had to do. Send him home! Pronto. Before he regained use of that arm and used it to snare her.

Chase could see her retreating from him. The wild tingling in his arm was being echoed elsewhere in his body, protesting the sudden cut-off of their embrace. Of all the times for him to get clumsy.

"Time for you to go." Nicole shoved an armload of books at him. "Take these with you."

"That's not necessary."

"Yes, it is." She couldn't believe that moments before she'd been wantonly draped across his lap, kissing him as if there were no tomorrow. The realization of how deeply she'd been affected by Chase's kiss only served to reinforce Nicole's belief that he was dangerous—*extremely* dangerous to her peace of mind. "The fun and games are over for tonight, Detective."

Chase knew there was a time to fight and a time to leave well enough alone. He opted for the latter. "There's always tomorrow," he murmured, his gaze silently promising her he'd be back.

Nicole didn't breathe easily until he'd left. Locking the back door after him, she sank down onto one of the nearby straight-backed kitchen chairs and willed her knees to stop shaking.

"Now what are you going to do?" she asked herself, her voice bouncing around the empty kitchen. "He'll be back. He knows he's got you right where he wants you. Well, not *right* where he wants me, but darn close. Too close."

Chase was taking over... taking over her thoughts, her dreams, her life. She needed a distraction. She needed reinforcements.

An idea was coming to her....

With one hand Nicole reached for the telephone on the wall while using her other to grab her phone book. Seconds later she was dialing.

"Grant, it's me, Nicole Larson. I hope it's not too late for me to be calling."

"Not at all." Grant's voice was friendly, but not laced with hidden meaning the way *some* men's voices were, Nicole noted. Good. She didn't want hidden meanings and seductive promises. She wanted intelligent conversation and common interests.

"I'm glad to hear from you," Grant continued. "To what do I owe this pleasure? Business or..."

"It's not business," Nicole replied, hoping he'd take the hint.

He did. "By any chance, could this call mean that you've reconsidered my invitation for us to go out together?"

"That's exactly what it means," Nicole confirmed, relieved that he was so perceptive—unlike *some* men.

"Great. When?"

"Would tomorrow evening be too soon?" she inquired.

"Not at all," Grant assured her. "Would six be convenient for you?"

A man who considered her convenience for a change. How refreshing! She was definitely doing the right thing. "That would be fine. Could you pick me up at the library?"

"Certainly."

"Thanks, Grant."

"Thank *you*," he gallantly countered. "I'll see you tomorrow."

Hanging up the phone, Nicole allowed herself one final triumphant thought. Put that in your pipe and smoke it, Detective Know-it-All, Kisses-like-the-Devil, Ellis!

Seven

Nicole prepared for work with extra care the next morning. For one thing, she didn't want any signs of her restless night showing. That meant using more foundation than usual to erase, or at least cover up, some of the shadows under her eyes.

She didn't want Chase seeing any vulnerability on her part. She didn't want him knowing she'd been up half the night. And she certainly didn't want him knowing about the very intimate dreams she'd had when she finally *had* fallen asleep.

Chase might have won the skirmish last night, slipping past her defenses—practically melting them altogether with the provocative heat of his caresses. But the war wasn't over yet. It was time to bring out the heavy artillery.

Hence her dress. It was slightly more elegant than something she would normally have worn to work. After all, Nicole never knew when she'd be called upon to scrounge around for some hard-to-reach book so her clothes had to be practical as well as professional. Something was always cropping up—she just didn't want it to be the hemline of her skirt!

The bottom line was that the electric blue dress not only looked good, but also made her *feel* good. Confident. Like she knew what she was doing.

Nicole needed that today. Needed that extra dose of self-confidence. Because she wasn't about to allow herself to become just another notch in Chase Ellis's bedpost, regardless of how he might tempt her.

"So his kisses defy description," Nicole resolutely lectured her reflection in the mirror. "He didn't get that way by accident!" She waved her mascara wand for emphasis. "He got that way by practicing. On women. Lots of them, no doubt."

Simply put, the man was impossible. He thought he could waltz into her life, straight into her bed, and waltz right back out again. He certainly wasn't the type to make a commitment.

Not that she wanted him to. They had nothing in common. He had no respect for her profession, or for much of anything that she could see.

It was time she took action, time she fought back. Which was precisely why she was going out with Grant Myers tonight.

In agreeing to go out with Grant, Nicole hoped to prove two things to Chase. The first was that she wasn't under Chase's spell, regardless of *how* incredible his kisses were. And the second was that all male librarians were *not* nerds.

Grant Myers certainly wasn't. A library administrator for the regional library system, Grant was quite good-looking in a smooth *GQ* kind of way. She should have accepted his earlier invitations to go out, she chastised herself. Who needed raw excitement? Not her.

Nicole had been through the wringer once. With Johnny. She wasn't making the mistake of getting tangled up again with a man who loved trouble.

To her relief, Chase wasn't scheduled to come in to work until noon. That meant she only had six hours to get through, and hopefully she'd be able to avoid him for at least part of that time.

He caught up with her before long, however, cornering her during one of the brief moments she was in her office.

"I just wanted to remind you..." The look Chase gave her clearly implied that he was reminding her about last night and the passionate embrace they'd shared.

Although Nicole resolutely looked him straight in the eye, she could feel her face getting warm.

"Remind you about Dayton," Chase continued. "You mentioned yesterday something about needing..." There was needing and there was *needing*. She knew which kind he was talking about! "Umm—" He cleared his throat as if he was nervous, which she knew darn well he wasn't. "—About needing my help with shifting some books."

Nicole had forgotten all about that. She'd had other things on her mind.

Checking the schedule posted to the wall above her desk, she said, "I asked Dayton to come in at eight-thirty this evening."

"Fine."

"I'm leaving at six tonight," she informed him.

"Really? Got a hot date?" he inquired with jovial mockery.

"Yes, I do," Nicole confirmed with a smile. Feeling incredibly pleased with herself, she sashayed out of her office.

* * *

Chase told himself that it was no business of his who the librarian went out with. He was just here to do his job, not to get involved.

Besides, she was probably just talking through her hat, throwing smoke at him to obscure the fact that she'd been an equal participant in their embrace last night. Not that it mattered one way or the other. He had his hands full with this case and he needed to keep his attention on it.

With that thought in mind, Chase attended to business. "Frieda, you're just the woman I want to talk to."

"Is something wrong?"

"Not at all. I just wanted to say..." Remembering he was supposed to be shy, he stuttered a bit before continuing. "W-well, I couldn't help but notice that you seem a little uncomfortable with my name. It's happened before," he reassured her when she looked embarrassed. "If it would make you feel better, you can call me Al. It's less of a mouthful than Mr. Hoffstedder."

"I don't know." Frieda looked doubtful. "You don't seem like an Al to me. No, Alvin suits you best. I've gotten over my initial reaction... I just feel badly for having made a thing about it in the first place."

"No problem," Chase assured her. "Working with people a lot the way you do, I'll bet you've run across your share of strange names." He wanted to make her feel at ease before he pumped her for information.

"Yes. Some strange people, too."

"You must know a lot about the folks in this town," he casually noted.

"You could say that," Frieda agreed.

"Every community is different, but they all have things in common. There will always be those who drink, who cheat on their spouses, who gamble..." He deliberately let his voice trail off suggestively.

Frieda turned pale. "I don't know anything about that," she said quickly, too quickly.

Her reaction fit in with what Chase already knew about Frieda from the information he'd gathered so far. Frieda's husband, a retired engineer, enjoyed a weekly trip to Davenport to partake in the gambling on the riverboat there. In between trips, the man frequented a high-stakes bingo game at a local pub. It was enough to make Frieda one of the prime suspects.

The problem was that he had several prime suspects here. Anna, the children's librarian, had a brother with an arrest record for extortion and racketeering. Michelle, the young single mother, was up to her eyes in debt with creditors dunning her daily. He didn't know much about Dayton yet, but he planned on finding out what he could that evening. Then he had to research the three teenage pages who reshelved the books after they'd been returned. He didn't plan on overlooking anyone.

The only reason that Nicole was above suspicion was that she'd been out of town at a library conference when this whole thing had started. And, as he'd told her earlier, her record was clear. Nothing suspicious there, except for the way she made his blood boil when she finally *did* decide to kiss him back.

Forget about it, Chase told himself. Still, it wouldn't hurt to do a little investigating...

"So, do you know anything about Nicole's big date tonight?" he asked Frieda, who looked relieved at the change of subject.

"No, I don't."

Chase suspected that Nicole had just made up that story to pay him back for kissing her last night. It was something a woman would do, rather than accept that she was attracted to him. Always wanting to complicate things, that was a woman for you.

The next time Chase saw Nicole, he made a point of referring to her plans for the evening. "I hope you have fun on your big date tonight."

The look he gave her was brief and subtle so that no one else would notice, but Nicole did. She read his visual message loud and clear. He didn't think she really had a date!

"Thank you, Alvin. I plan on having a *very* good time tonight," Nicole replied, reminding herself that *she* who laughs last, laughs best.

The library was quiet for the rest of the afternoon. Chase spent the better part of an hour helping a student who wanted to learn how to use WordPerfect on the computer in conference room one. By the time he returned to the circulation desk, Frieda had left for the day and Michelle had taken her place.

"Nicole, there's someone here to see you," he heard Michelle tell her.

"I'll be right there," Nicole replied from her office. A pair of pearl earrings, a matching necklace in the unbuttoned V-neckline of her blue dress, and a pair of dressy pumps turned what had been a stylish work outfit into a classy evening ensemble.

Chase noticed the difference. He also noticed the preppy-looking guy in the tailored suit waiting for her.

Still think I'm making this up? she silently challenged Chase with one meaningful look.

Nicole made the introductions. "You already know Michelle. And this is Alvin Hoffstedder, our new circulation librarian. Alvin, this is Grant Myers. He's a library administrator with the regional library system."

"Glad to meet you, Alvin."

"Same here." For the first time since donning his role as Alvin, Chase felt uncomfortable with his choice of clothing. He uneasily fiddled with the stupid bow tie he was wearing before realizing what he was doing. He immediately stopped.

Nicole hid her smile. This was turning out just as she'd hoped. She couldn't have come up with a better representative than Grant. He could well have been an attorney or a doctor. There was nothing the least bit nerdy about Grant. That was one of the reasons she wanted Chase to meet him. To prove that male librarians did not all look like nerds!

She also wanted to prove to him that she was seeing other men in a social way. Dating them. So he wouldn't think that she was home waiting or thinking about him.

The final thing she wanted to prove was to herself. And that was that she wasn't falling under Chase's dangerous spell. Because getting the least bit involved with him was asking for a heartache. Nicole had gone that route before. She had no desire to experience that kind of trauma again.

"If you're ready, Nicole, we've got reservations at six-thirty," Grant said.

"Of course."

"You two going out to dinner to discuss library business?" Chase asked.

"Nope." With a breezy smile, Nicole put her hand on Grant's arm. "I'm ready."

It required every ounce of Chase's acting ability not to glare and frown at the happy couple as they left the library. This Grant guy could prove to be an unexpected fly in the ointment. Here Chase thought things were moving right along with Nicole and now she deliberately flaunted this guy in his face.

Chase had no doubt that Nicole's actions had been deliberate. She'd gotten pleasure out of needling him. She'd also made a point of informing him that the perfect Grant Myers was a librarian. One of her *own* kind. Smooth. Polished. Chase had an unreasonable desire to rearrange the guy's face.

He told himself that it was no skin off his nose if she wanted to go out with other guys. Then why did it bother him so much? Because she was an incredibly sexy, passionate woman with the courage to stand up to him? Because she was a fascinating, challenging puzzle he couldn't solve? Or because when she smiled at him he felt like he'd won the lotto, big time?

"Have Nicole and Grant known each other long?" Chase casually asked Michelle, telling himself his interest was strictly professional while mocking his own self-deception.

"A little over a year," Michelle replied.

"They've been going out that long?" Chase wasn't pleased. This sounded more serious than he'd first thought.

Michelle shook her head. "No, not at all. I think Grant was interested, but Nicole never accepted his invitations before. I'm glad to see that she finally has."

"You are?"

"Absolutely. She deserves to be happy."

"What makes you think Grant would make her happy?" Chase demanded.

"Who wouldn't be happy with a great-looking guy like him?" Michelle countered.

Something about the look on his face must have reflected his displeasure.

"It's all right, Alvin." Michelle patted his arm reassuringly. "Not everyone judges a book by its cover. I'm sure there's a woman for you out there... somewhere."

Yeah, Chase noted on a disgruntled note, there was a woman for him all right... and she'd just walked out on another's guy's arm!

"I'm glad you called," Grant said as he gallantly pulled out the chair for Nicole to sit on. The restaurant he'd chosen specialized in French cuisine and the decor was appropriately continental. Fine china. Fresh flowers. Discreet classical music in the background. Very elegant.

"I'm glad, too," Nicole agreed. It was nice to be able to enjoy a man's company without that constant hum of attraction racing through her system every two seconds.

"Your new librarian seems like a real throwback to the old days," Grant noted.

"He's got excellent references," Nicole felt compelled to say.

"I'm sure he does. You wouldn't have hired him otherwise."

"No, I wouldn't."

"It was generous of you to hire him despite the bow tie," Grant said in a teasing voice.

"Yes, I thought so, too. But I hope we won't be spending the entire evening talking about the newest member of the library's staff," Nicole added. After all, she'd come out to get away from Chase and his alter ego Alvin.

"We won't mention him again," Grant promised.

And they didn't.

After Grant had placed their orders, raspberry chicken for her and veal for him, Nicole was surprised when someone lightly touched her shoulder. For one instant she thought Chase had followed them. She wouldn't put it past him. But it was only Leo.

"Nicole, how nice to see you," he said.

"Leo! What a surprise." She hadn't expected to run into him here. This restaurant was fairly pricey.

Leo seemed to guess her thoughts. "I know, this isn't really my kind of place, is it? But I'm meeting my cousin's husband Eddie for dinner here, and he's treating. There he is now." Leo waved as a man entered the restaurant.

Nicole automatically turned to look at the new arrival. He appeared to be Leo's complete opposite—a smooth-looking, flashy dresser. She imagined that when the two men were side by side, they must be like day and night. Complete opposites. But then, they *were* only related by marriage.

"Well, I'd better go," Leo said. "Enjoy your dinner."

"Who were you talking to?" Eddie suspiciously demanded the second Leo joined him.

"Nicole. She's the head librarian at..."

"Librarian! Are you nuts?" Eddie hissed. "Get over here!" He dragged Leo outside, not stopping until they reached his car. "Don't you have any brains at all?"

"What's the problem?" Leo asked in confusion.

"What's the problem? The problem is that I have to work with nitwits like you. Geez." Eddie kicked the car's tires in disgust. "If only I didn't have to hire family I'd be much better off."

"I appreciate the work," Leo assured him.

"Fine. Then do it right and don't take stupid risks like talking to the librarian."

"I've always talked to her. She'll think it strange if I stop."

"You *are* strange, Leo," Eddie retorted before getting into his car.

"Does this mean we're not having dinner tonight?" Leo asked through the open window.

"It means I don't want to hear about any problems."

"There won't be any problems, Eddie."

"There better not be."

"What a strangle little man," Grant was saying.

"Leo? He's really very sweet. And very intelligent. He invents things. He's one of our patrons at the library."

"Here we are, talking about the library again," Grant noted wryly.

"You're right. No more talk of work." Because work was tied to Chase and Nicole refused to even think about him.

And she was pleased to find that in Grant's company she was able to forget about Chase—for the time being, anyway.

But when they got home, and Grant gallantly kissed her good-night, Nicole's memories of Chase came back with a vengeance. Unwanted comparisons came to mind. This was bland. This wasn't right. She quickly broke off the brief contact.

"Maybe we can do this again," Grant said.

"Maybe we can," Nicole said wistfully, hoping that there would come a day when she'd be able to forget Chase for longer than a mere five hours.

She'd just unlocked her door and turned to wave Grant goodbye as he drove away, when she caught a hint of movement out of the corner of her eye.

"What a touching moment," Chase murmured from the sheltering boughs of a large blue spruce edging her front porch. "But on a scale of one to ten, I'd only give the guy a four for his performance, though. He gets points for being smooth, but I had to mark him down for not having enough creativity in his program."

Nicole stared at Chase's casually lounging figure in disbelief. "What are you doing here?"

"Waiting for you."

"Spying on me is more likely."

"Give me a break! You think I have nothing better to do than stand out here spying on you and Sir Galahad?" Without waiting to be invited, Chase followed her inside, closing the door behind him. "Watching the Disney Channel is more exciting than you two are."

"And I suppose you're an expert?"

"At watching kid's programs, no."

No doubt the R-rated adult cable channel was more up his alley! "Some people aren't looking for excitement," she loftily informed him.

"Good. Because you're not going to find it with that guy."

"I had a wonderful time with him," Nicole retorted.

"Maybe you did. Until he kissed you," Chase astutely added.

Furious that he'd read her so correctly, Nicole turned her back on him. "You don't know anything about it!"

"I know that when you kiss me, you close your eyes and make these incredibly sexy little murmurs."

"In your dreams, maybe," she retorted.

"No. In my arms."

A second later he had her there, wrapped in his embrace.

Just as she parted her lips to voice her protest, Chase swooped down and covered her mouth with his. The slant of his approach ensured complete possession. Instant intimacy. Familiar fantasies. The sleekness of his tongue tempting her, tempting her...

Nicole tried to hang on to her self-control, but it was hopeless. Pleasure this intense wasn't meant to be fought. It was simply meant to be.

Which was just as well because there was no denying the provocative demand of Chase's kiss. She couldn't resist. She didn't want to. She wanted...oh, how he made her want things she hadn't wanted in years!

Possession. Raw ecstasy. Gratification. His mouth engulfed hers in a turbulent exchange that left her breathless with desire. Chase tightened his hold on her, almost imprinting his hard angles onto her soft curves.

His passion didn't intimidate her, because she felt the same raging need that he did. The need to be close, to taste, to explore, to touch.

Her arms slid around his waist, her fingers seeking out the hem of his dark T-shirt, impatiently tugging it from the waistband of his jeans. His skin was warm to her touch as she explored the curve of his spine, surveying this wondrously powerful male body pressed so close to hers. She was entranced with the ripple of his muscles beneath her fingertips, while relishing her newfound freedom to touch him as she pleased. It was exhilarating. It was exciting.

She didn't even realize that he'd unbuttoned the front of her dress until she felt the warmth of his hand on her bare skin. Compared to the hungry fierceness of his mouth, his fingers were infinitely gentle as they skimmed over her collarbone before moving downward to the rounded swell of her breast. His touch lingered along the line where silky lace met equally silky skin.

Ever so slowly, he stole his way beneath the shielding lace of her bra until he reached the firm crest of one breast. When his fingertips brushed her there, Nicole went weak at the knees—the pleasure was that intense.

"Oh, yes, yes..." Nicole murmured her husky approval against his mouth, which was hovering mere millimeters above hers. He savored her panting sighs, incorporating them into the rapidly escalating passion of their kiss.

Nicole matched him move for move, her tongue sliding over his. She drank in the darkly potent kisses he was plying her with, becoming addicted to their taste and texture.

Wet heat. Everywhere.

Chase slid one hand around to the small of her back, cupping her there and lifting her upward against him. His hips moved against hers with unmistakable intent. The rhythmic motion was wildly exciting.

Nicole felt as if she'd been tossed into the middle of a volcano. A virgin maiden given up as sacrifice to the vengeful gods. Only this vengeful god had the power to make her believe that this was exactly where she should be. This was no sacrifice, this was destiny. It was what she wanted, what she needed, what she had to have.

This fire. This molten stirring deep within her. Red hot. Elemental. Primitive.

Out of control. Chase felt completely out of control. This never happened to him. She had some kind of power over him. An ancient, uncanny feminine power. Who was seducing whom? he hazily wondered before abruptly setting her free.

"I don't know what's going on here," Chase muttered, "but I don't like it." A second later he was gone, leaving a bemused Nicole behind.

Eight

After Chase's abrupt departure, Nicole was a mass of jangled nerves and raging hormones. She'd changed into a cotton sleep shirt, but couldn't sleep—and once again it was Chase's fault. Why had he left like that? Was this some new game he was playing? After further thought, she didn't think so.

No, there had been something new added to the equation tonight. For the first time, Nicole began to feel as if she weren't the only susceptible one. She wasn't sure whether to be pleased or shaken with this latest development.

The possibility that Chase wasn't simply flirting, wasn't just fooling around in that devilish way of his, carried an element of risk all its own. Before it had been a game—one she'd been able to dismiss because she knew he'd merely been playing with her. But maybe this wasn't just a game for him. Maybe he was as unavoidably drawn to her as she was to him.

Why did that scare her? The fact that he might feel something, too, didn't mean that he was declaring undying love for her or anything of the kind. She didn't even want him to. Did she?

Nicole was so confused! She needed to talk to someone or go crazy. So she called her sister in San Francisco. It was two hours earlier there, Diane would still be up.

"Hi, there," Nicole said, wrapping the phone coil around her index finger. "It's me."

"Hi, Nicole. It's good to hear from you."

After catching up with family news, Diane said, "Okay, what's wrong?"

"How could you tell something was wrong?"

"I'm your big sister. It's my job to know when something is wrong."

"If I tell you about this, you have to swear you won't tell a soul."

"Who am I going to tell?"

"I mean it, Diane. I probably shouldn't be telling anyone, even you, about this, but if I don't talk to someone I'm going to go crazy."

"So tell me already."

"Swear you won't tell another living soul. Not even your cat."

"Cross my heart and hope to die, stick a needle in my eye," Diane chanted, as they had when they had been kids.

"Okay, here's the deal. There's this man at work..."

"There is?"

"Would you let me finish, please? Anyway there's this man at work and then there's this man..."

"Wait, there are two men?" Diane inserted.

"Yes and no. I'm not explaining this very clearly..."

"You can say that again."

"It would help if you wouldn't interrupt me every two seconds," Nicole said with sisterly exasperation.

IT'S FUN! IT'S FREE!
AND IT COULD MAKE YOU A

MILLIONAIRE

If you've ever played scratch-off lottery tickets, you should be familiar with how our games work. On each of the first four tickets (numbered 1 to 4 in the upper right) there are Pink Metallic Strips to scratch off.

Using a coin, do just that—carefully scratch the PINK strips to reveal how much each ticket could be worth if it is a winning ticket. Tickets could be worth from $100.00 to $1,000,000.00 in lifetime money.

Note, also, that each of your 4 tickets has a unique sweepstakes Lucky Number . . . and that's 4 chances for a **BIG WIN**!

FREE BOOKS!

At the same time you play your tickets for big prizes, you are invited to play ticket #5 for the chance to get one or more free books from Silhouette®. We give away free books to introduce readers to the benefits of the Silhouette Reader Service™.

Accepting the free book(s) places you under no obligation to buy anything! You may keep your free book(s) and return the accompanying statement marked ''cancel.'' But if we don't hear from you, then every month, we'll deliver 6 of the newest Silhouette Desire® novels right to your door. You'll pay the low subscriber price of just $2.49* each—a saving of 40¢ apiece off the cover price! And there's no charge for shipping and handling! You may cancel at any time.

Of course, you may play ''THE BIG WIN'' without requesting any free book(s) by scratching tickets #1 through #4 only. But remember, that first shipment of one or more books is FREE!

PLUS A FREE GIFT!

One more thing, when you accept the free book(s) on ticket #5, you are also entitled to play ticket #6, which is GOOD FOR A GREAT GIFT! Like the book(s), this gift is totally free and yours to keep as thanks for giving our Reader Service a try!

So scratch off the PINK STRIPS on all your BIG WIN tickets and send for everything today! You've got nothing to lose and everything to gain!

Here are your BIG WIN Game Tickets, worth from $100.00 to $1,000,000.00 each. Scratch off the PINK METALLIC STRIP on each of your Sweepstakes tickets to see what you could win and mail your entry right away. (SEE OFFICIAL RULES IN BACK OF BOOK FOR DETAILS!)

This could be your lucky day - GOOD LUCK!

THE BIG WIN

TICKET 1
Scratch PINK METALLIC STRIP to reveal potential value of this ticket if it is a winning ticket. Return all game tickets intact.
LUCKY NUMBER
1B 128790

TICKET 2.
Scratch PINK METALLIC STRIP to reveal potential value of this ticket if it is a winning ticket. Return all game tickets intact.
LUCKY NUMBER
4K 116318

TICKET 3
Scratch PINK METALLIC STRIP to reveal potential value of this ticket if it is a winning ticket. Return all game tickets intact.
LUCKY NUMBER
7B 169994

TICKET 4
Scratch PINK METALLIC STRIP to reveal potential value of this ticket if it is a winning ticket. Return all game tickets intact.
LUCKY NUMBER
2X 109378

FREE BOOKS

TICKET 5
We're giving away brand new books to selected individuals. Scratch PINK METALLIC STRIP for number of free books you will receive.
AUTHORIZATION CODE
130107-742

FREE GIFT

TICKET 6
We have an outstanding added gift for you if you are accepting our free books. Scratch PINK METALLIC STRIP to reveal gift.
AUTHORIZATION CODE
130107-742

YES! Enter my Lucky Numbers in THE BIG WIN Sweepstakes and when winners are selected, tell me if I've won any prize. If PINK METALLIC STRIP is scratched off on ticket #5, I will also receive one or more FREE Silhouette Desire® novels along with the FREE GIFT on ticket #6, as explained on the opposite page.

(U-SIL-D-04/92) 225 CIS ADPW

NAME _____

ADDRESS _____ APT. _____

CITY _____ STATE _____ ZIP _____

Offer limited to one per household and not valid to current Silhouette Desire subscribers.

© 1991 HARLEQUIN ENTERPRISES LIMITED.

FOLD AND DETACH ALONG THIS DOTTED LINE—RETURN ALL GAME TICKETS INTACT.

**Carefully detach card along dotted lines and mail today!
Play all your BIG WIN tickets and get everything you're
entitled to—including FREE BOOKS and a FREE GIFT!**

ALTERNATE MEANS OF ENTRY: Print your name and address on a 3″ × 5″
piece of plain paper and send to: Silhouette Reader Service,
3010 Walden Ave., P.O. Box 1867, Buffalo, NY 14269-1867

NO POSTAGE
NECESSARY
IF MAILED
IN THE
UNITED STATES

BUSINESS REPLY MAIL
FIRST CLASS MAIL   PERMIT NO. 717   BUFFALO, NY

POSTAGE WILL BE PAID BY ADDRESSEE

SILHOUETTE READER SERVICE
3010 WALDEN AVE
PO BOX 1867
BUFFALO NY 14240-9952

"Okay, okay. Go ahead. Take your time. Just try to be coherent."

"I'll start over. For reasons I can't go into right now, someone in an official capacity has been called upon to do some work in the library. What I mean is that someone not normally in the library profession is temporarily filling that position. Anyway, we're sort of... required... to work together. Only he's not really an employee of mine. Are you following me?"

"I'm trying to," Diane retorted. "Go on."

"At work this man is very bookwormish. But he's not really like that at all. He's really this extremely sexy guy who won't stop flirting with me. I mean, I'm the only one who knows what he's really like and I don't really know him that well. I only know that when he kisses me... we're talking major earthquakes here."

Diane groaned. "Remember who you're speaking to and please don't mention earthquakes. I survived the big one here in 1989."

"Sorry. Anyway, I thought this guy was just amusing himself at my expense... you know, trying to rile the lady librarian, but then tonight...he kissed me...and...I don't know. For the first time he seemed as shaken as I was. Now I don't know what to think."

"Me, either," Diane cheerfully concurred.

"You're a big help!"

"Oh, you wanted *help*. I get it. You've met this new man in your life and you're attracted to him. At first you don't think he's really attracted to you, but now it sounds like he could be. What's the problem?"

"The problem is that this man courts trouble. No, let me revise that statement. He doesn't merely court trouble, he delights in instigating it. He's arrogant, self-centered, and he's got a reckless streak in him a mile wide."

"Ah, now I get it. This is about Johnny, isn't it?" Diane noted astutely. She was the only one in Nicole's family who knew the true depth of her relationship with Johnny.

"You noticed the similarities, huh?" Nicole replied. "So did I. That's why I didn't want to get involved. As you know, the one time I let loose and rebelled, it was deadly."

"I've told you before that what happened to Johnny wasn't your fault."

"I know you have. And I wish I could believe you, I really do. But deep inside me there's this guilt. And fear."

"Is that why you've been very careful not to let that rebellious side of yourself out again?"

"What are you talking about?"

"You're a respectable librarian now, very conscientious. There's no sign of that college girl who ran around with a biker crowd."

"You make it sound like I was hanging out with members of Hell's Angels," Nicole protested.

"You know what I mean."

"I know. And you're right," Nicole acknowledged slowly. "I guess I've deliberately cultivated an image of being responsible and cautious. I haven't become a doormat, though. I still fight for what I believe in."

"I know you do. Where your work is concerned, you're very passionate. But what about the rest of the time? I've been telling you for years that your classy demeanor keeps men at bay. Makes them maintain a chivalrous distance."

"And what's wrong with a chivalrous distance?" Nicole demanded.

"Nothing for someone who really *is* staid and cautious, not merely cultivating an image."

Nicole was silent a moment as her sister's words sank in. Then she sighed. "What's wrong with me? Why do I seem to be attracted to these dangerous types? To the guys in black leather, the bad boys. The raw and untamed ones."

"The sexy ones," her sister inserted.

"Right."

"Who isn't attracted to them?" Diane countered.

"I'm not just attracted to them. They also scare me," Nicole quietly admitted.

"Have you ever considered the possibility that maybe it's not the men you're afraid of, it's what they represent?"

"What do you mean?"

"I mean that the one time you allowed yourself to get intimately involved with a man, he ended up dying right in front of you. And while it was in no way your fault, the experience is bound to have left its mark on you. And maybe that mark is that you're afraid of feeling that way again—that uncontrolled, that wild."

"So you think it's some kind of sexual hang-up, is that what you're telling me?"

"Not entirely, no. But it is something for you to think about."

And think about it Nicole did. It seemed as if since she'd met Chase she'd done nothing but think about sex. About what it would be like with him. And that wasn't like her at all. At least it wasn't like the *her* she'd become. It was more like the wilder more rebellious *her* she'd once been. Right now Chase had her so mixed-up she wasn't sure *who* she was anymore!

He had no business chasing after the librarian, Chase chastised himself as he walked into his half-empty apartment. He had a case to work on. This was no time to be fooling around. He needed to concentrate on nailing the head of the gambling ring and getting out of there. Before he did something stupid. Like care. That would not be a wise move.

Chase dropped his keys onto the table, which did dual service as both a desk and a table. Compared to the warmth and comfort of Nicole's house, his apartment looked bleak and barren. It had never bothered him before. He'd liked the emptiness. Made it easier to clean.

The ringing phone interrupted his reflections on the state of his apartment, and his life. Chief Straud was on the line.

"I've been trying to reach you all evening," the chief said.

Chase was immediately all business. "Something up?"

"No. I just wanted to check in with you. As I said, I tried calling earlier, but you were out."

As in out of my mind, out of my league, Chase noted derisively. He should never have gone over to Nicole's house. He should never have waited for her and he should certainly never have followed her inside and kissed her.

"So how are things going?" Chief Straud cheerfully inquired.

"Oh, dandy. Just dandy," Chase muttered.

"And Nicole?"

"She's just dandy, too." And she'd left him feeling achingly randy.

Some of that restless discomfort must have come across in Chase's voice because the chief asked, "You two having any problems?"

"What makes you ask that?"

"When I first introduced you two, you ended up staring daggers into each other. It wasn't exactly a congenial meeting as I recall."

"Yeah, well I'm not exactly the congenial type."

"I had heard that about you," Chief Straud admitted with a chuckle.

"So how much do you know about Nicole Larson?" Chase asked him.

"I've known her most of her life."

"Comes from a good family, I bet."

"The best," the chief replied.

Figured. She wasn't the kind of woman a man just slept with once or twice. No fly-by-night rolls in the hay. No one-night stands. She was classy. And sexy. An unlucky combination in Chase's experience.

"You still there, Chase?"

"Yeah, I'm still here." Still aching with unsatisfied desire. Chase shifted, trying to find a more comfortable position in a wooden chair that was as hard as he was.

"Nicole told me things were going fine."

"When did she tell you that?" Chase demanded.

"When I talked to her a few days ago."

"Did she say anything else?"

"She mentioned that you never tell her anything. I assured her that that was for her own protection. She seemed a little distracted, though. You wouldn't happen to know anything about that, would you?"

"She seems fine to me." Too fine. Too tempting. Too provocative.

"Good. Because I wouldn't want to see her hurt, if you get my drift. As I said, I've known her since she was a little girl and I wouldn't take too kindly to hearing that she'd been distressed in any way."

Here it came again. Once again Chase was being warned off—this time by an overprotective father figure instead of the real thing. He felt cursed. He felt frustrated. He felt like hanging up on the kindhearted police chief. "Nicole is a big girl," he said curtly. "I don't think you have to worry about her."

Chase *was* beginning to worry about himself, however. Because he had this sinking feeling that if he wasn't very careful, Nicole Larson could ultimately prove to be his downfall. Since the breakup of his engagement, he'd managed to keep his emotional distance from other women, flirting but never falling for them.

The flirting had come easily with Nicole. The problem was that Chase was afraid falling for her would come too damn easily, as well. And given his previous experience with his ex-fiancée, that was definitely an unnerving proposition.

Nicole was relieved to have the next two days, Saturday and Sunday, off. It gave her a chance to mow the lawn, do her laundry, and run a dozen errands in town. It did not give her a chance to forget about Chase, however. He was in her thoughts every step of the way. She stopped at Berhren's Hardware Store to replace a broken hammer and ended up wondering how Chase would look wearing one of the nifty tool belts displayed nearby.

She paid her electric bill two doors down at the corner drugstore and—for the first time ever—noticed the display of condoms located nearby. How long had those been there? She'd been paying her utility bills at this drugstore for years and had never noticed the display before. Now she felt as if they might jump off the racks at her as she stood there fanning herself with her electric bill, trying to look natural...and fervently wishing the line was shorter so she could just pay her bill and leave.

Unfortunately, one of the joys of living in a small town was also one of its curses. Almost everyone knew her, either from her childhood years of growing up in Oak Heights or from her position as librarian. So naturally at least four people commented to her about how flushed she looked standing there in line.

"You look warm," said the woman who'd given Nicole piano lessons when she was ten.

"Hope you're not coming down with something," said the woman who'd worked at the Tivoli Theater since Nicole was twelve.

"Looks like you got a touch of sunburn," noted the wife of one of the library board members.

"Global warming," Mr. Kedzie, the town doomsayer predicted from near the head of the line. "Pretty soon we're all going to just burn up and that will be the end of it."

Nicole felt like burning up... from embarrassment... right there and then. Once she finally got to the head of the line and paid her bill, Nicole made a hasty getaway while silently cursing her creamy complexion for advertising her emotions like a neon light. While no one could have known the source of her embarrassment, *she'd* known.

Her last stop was the dime store. Oak Heights was one of the few places that still had a bona fide dime store left in its two-block-long downtown section. Shopping malls had taken their place in most other suburbs. Nicole had always liked the dime store and its Old World ambiance. The place made her feel as if she were stepping back in time. But not today. Today she realized where Chase had gotten those bow ties of his. Right here.

She stopped in front of a selection covering the muddier hues of the rainbow. She supposed she should have been glad he didn't get the grimy gray one with pea-green shamrocks on it. Having forgotten what she'd come into the store for in the first place, Nicole left in a hurry. But she couldn't escape her thoughts of Chase, which continued to hound her even in her sleep that night.

It was almost a relief to return to work Monday morning, where she could at least face her nemesis head-on. Nicole got her first inkling of change when she discovered that Alvin was not wearing his trademark mismatched shirt and bow tie. Instead he'd traded it in for a navy cotton sweater vest, a light blue short-sleeved shirt and a burgundy tie.

It was a subtle change, not enough to make anyone suspicious that he really was a wolf in lamb's clothing. He was just a better-looking lamb. Nicole noticed that right away.

Over the next two days, other people began to take notice as well.

"Alvin looks better today, don't you think?" Frieda noted to Nicole.

You should see him in black jeans and a black T-shirt, Nicole thought to herself. While she saw Alvin every day at work, she hadn't seen Chase since the night she'd come home from her date with Grant and he'd kissed her. No, that seemed too tame a description of what he'd done to her. He'd not only *kissed* her, he'd caressed her, tempted her, driven her to the very edge . . .

Nicole didn't even realize she was fanning herself with a catalog card until she caught Frieda watching her.

"It's warm in here, isn't it?" Nicole noted casually. Since they were in the beginning stages of what promised to be a steamy heat wave, she at least had some basis for her comment. The rising temperatures outside weren't responsible for the sultry way she felt, however. The heat was internal and high enough to make her feel feverish. Indeed, Chase had become like a fever that had gotten into her bloodstream and was raging through her system.

She still didn't know why he'd left so suddenly the way he had four nights ago. He'd been avoiding her since then. And strangely enough, that gave her hope. Because maybe it meant he'd been as shaken up as she was by the passion that had flared up between them. Since then she'd caught him, once or twice, looking at her in a new way, as if seeing her for the very first time.

"I think he's been taking our advice," Frieda continued.

"Who is?" Nicole asked absently, her attention distracted with thoughts of Chase.

"Alvin. It's amazing what just a change of clothing can do, isn't it? I mean without that bow tie and with his hair not slicked back so severely, he doesn't resemble a nerd at all."

You've got that right, Nicole silently noted.

"I'll bet if he got contacts and got a little more self-confidence, he might be quite good looking," Frieda added.

A little more self-confidence? The man had more than enough for two men as it was!

Frieda wasn't the only one to notice Alvin's changed appearance. Later that afternoon when Michelle took over at the desk, she commented on it, too. But when Anna came into her office and voiced her opinion, Nicole had had enough. "I know, I know. Alvin's taken everyone's advice," Nicole said. "I've heard it already."

"Did you hear that now the kids thinks he looks like that guy on *Quantum Leap?* A preppy intellectual type. He's got a gaggle of twelve-year-old girls asking him about quantum physics. You may have a heartthrob on your hands here," Anna said jokingly.

Tell me about it, Nicole brooded.

She told herself she should have been amused by the situation. But when the gaggle of twelve-year-olds were later joined by sexy sixteen-year-olds, she was not feeling particularly jocular about the situation. In fact, she was feeling downright...jealous.

This was the first time she'd seen Chase in action, albeit still under the guise of Alvin. There was a new level of flirtatiousness in his voice and manner, just a tad, not enough to make anyone suspicious that he'd transformed himself from a bookworm to a Don Juan. But it was done with a smoothness that told her that the flirtatiousness was very much part of his repertoire.

She'd suspected as much, but seeing him smiling at another female, even one who was merely sixteen, affected her. Of course, it *was* hard to beat the figure of a sixteen-year-old girl in a micro-mini. It was impossible not to be envious of their taut thighs and tiny hips. The svelte teenagers made Nicole feel like an overly ripe Mae West.

Professionally speaking she supposed she should have been pleased that Chase as Alvin was improving his image—and that of male librarians—moving away from being a dweeb toward…what? A sex symbol? Seeing the way the fawning girls were hanging on to his every word, Nicole wanted to go over and pour cold water on the teenagers' spiked hairdos.

Okay, so maybe she was overreacting here. What did it matter that the library presentation he was giving on Introduction to Computers had suddenly filled up all fifteen places in the past two hours? *She* was still the only one who knew what Alvin really looked like. She also knew how he kissed.

She didn't know what he thought, though. Maybe he was busy working on the case. There was no opportunity to ask.

One thing was certain: if those girls thought the new Alvin was appealing, they should get a load of Chase.

Nicole got a load of Chase later that night as he showed up unannounced at her back door. She'd just finished watching the ten o'clock news and was headed to the kitchen with an empty bowl of salad that had been her late-night dinner. The heat wave had indeed turned spring into summer overnight, with record-breaking temperatures that made Nicole wish she'd moved to Alaska with her youngest sister.

The window air conditioners she had at the house took the edge off the heat, but raised her electric bill to the point where she'd need to adhere to a stricter budget. Librarianship was not the best paying profession in the world. It ranked right up there with teaching. She was muttering about the overall inequity of that when she looked up and saw Chase's face through the glass windowpane on her back door.

Nicole did well. She didn't scream. She didn't even drop the bowl she was holding. She just walked over to the back door and let him in.

"Let me guess," she murmured. "You just happened to be in the neighborhood and decided to drop by."

"You got your locks fixed." He tapped the shiny new deadbolt approvingly before closing the door behind him. "Good."

"You came by for a security check? At this time of night?"

Chase wondered if he should have his *sanity* checked. After that last sizzling, mind-blowing kiss they'd shared, he should be keeping his distance. Instead here he was. He wasn't sure why. It had been a spur-of-the-moment idea. Not one of his best. "Never mind. This wasn't a good idea."

"That's never stopped you before," she couldn't resist pointing out.

"Funny. Very funny."

Nicole didn't want him leaving. Not now. Not when he'd finally shown up. "Did you eat any dinner?" she asked him.

He frowned, trying to remember.

"Would you like me to make you something? This time I've got roast beef," she added temptingly.

"I didn't come to mooch food off of you," Chase said.

"Consider it my way of assisting the police department. Instead of buying tickets to the pancake breakfast."

"Usually it's the fire department that has pancake breakfasts," he told her.

"Does that mean you're not interested?"

Oh, he was interested all right. And he shouldn't be. That was the problem. It never worked out when a guy like him got involved with a classy lady like Nicole. They always wanted to change him, tie him down with restrictions.

Still, now that he thought about it, he was starving. He'd had to grab his meals where he could the past few days.

Things were picking up with the case. The angle he was taking might be a bit unorthodox, but it had a good chance of working.

"You talked me into it. But you don't have to make it for me. I can help myself. Unless you object to my handling your crisper bin?" he inquired mockingly.

Part of her wanted him to handle anything he wanted, including *her!* The other saner part was trying to keep her on an even keel.

While her internal battle was being waged, Chase tilted his head to one side. "I hear voices," he said.

For a second she thought he was referring to the voices of caution and danger dueling in her head. Then she realized he meant the noise from the other room. "Oh that. I left the TV on."

"Oh." As Chase began constructing what promised to be another mega sandwich, he casually noted, "I meant to tell you, I had a long talk with Dayton the other night."

The night Chase had been waiting for her and kissed her senseless. It was no wonder to Nicole that the topic of Dayton had slipped her mind. Still, she felt remiss for not having brought up the subject herself.

"What did you say to him?" she asked Chase.

He looked up from the mustard design he was writing on his sandwich. "What do you mean?"

"To convince him to agree to my tutoring him. I've been trying for months and you talk to him and presto, he agrees."

"What can I say? I'm a smooth talker."

Chase was that, all right. And a lot more. But she wasn't through with the subject of Dayton yet. "And? Do you still think he's a suspect?"

"I think you may have been right about that." He added another layer of roast beef and two more slices of tomato to his culinary creation.

"*May* have been?"

"I'll agree that it's unlikely that Dayton is the one we're looking for."

"This is a first. You actually agreeing with me!"

"Don't let it go to your head," he warned her.

"I'll try not to," she promised mockingly.

In the end his sandwich looked so good that Nicole made one for herself, albeit a much smaller version. That salad she had had wasn't enough to keep a rabbit alive.

By mutual agreement, they ended up sitting on the couch in the living room eating their sandwiches while watching a late-night crime show.

Chase provided his own commentary about the policeman hero. "Did you hear that? No one uses perpetrator. We use *subject* or *suspect*. Never perpetrator. What a cliché."

"Bothers you when people have a mistaken view of your profession, does it?"

"You said it."

"Bothers me, too."

"Glad to hear it. You should write the TV show and complain," he said.

"I meant it bothers me when people have a mistaken view of *my* profession."

"By people, you mean me."

Since they had both polished off their respective sandwiches, Nicole stalled for time by offering him a peppermint candy from the crystal bowl she had on the coffee table. He took one, and so did she. That gave her the time she needed to cautiously phrase her reply. "I'm glad to see that you've... toned down your appearance—Alvin's appearance—to be more... realistic."

Chase popped the candy in his mouth before commenting. "The folks at the library seem to approve."

Now it was her turn to say, "By folks, you mean, sexy teenage girls."

"You don't sound real pleased," he noted with a grin.

"I'm glad they've finally decided to visit the library. Many of them haven't stepped foot inside the place since they were ten," she couldn't resist noting tartly.

"Consider it my way of assisting the library, instead of... what is it you do at the library for fund-raising?"

"Umm..." Since Nicole was in the middle of delicately slipping a candy between her lips, it took her a moment to answer. "We have an annual book sale of donated or out-of-date books."

"Fine. Consider it my way of assisting the library, instead of attending your book sale."

She wondered where he'd be by the time the library held its book sale at the end of the next month. She'd probably never know. He'd be out of her life by then. It was a sobering thought.

"Look at that!" Chase muttered in disgust. "No way you'd have a shoot-out in an enclosed underground rail station like that. Haven't these guys ever heard of ricocheting bullets?"

She wondered if Chase had been exposed to bullets, ricocheting or otherwise. The thought upset her so much that she reached for the remote control button and switched to a popular late-night talk show.

"What'd you do that for?" Chase demanded.

"The other show was too upsetting. For you, I mean. It seemed to be bothering you."

"So what? A lot of things bother me. Doesn't mean I give up on them."

Was he talking about the TV show or about them now? "If you don't give up, what do you do?" she asked him.

"I take action." He reached over to push the appropriate button on the remote control she still held in her hand.

So he *was* talking about the TV. Nicole sighed.

Then he turned to look at her. "*You* bother me," he murmured. "But I can't seem to give up on you, either."

"I bother you?" she questioned with some surprise.

He nodded.

"And you don't like to be the one being bothered, do you?" she noted with sudden insight. "You prefer being the one doing the bothering."

Nicole had hit the nail on the head. Chase didn't know whether to be pleased or disturbed at her accuracy in reading him so well. He only knew that, even though he should be staying as far as away as possible from Nicole, he couldn't resist being with her.

Kind of like him and caffeine, he reflected with a slightly self-derisive smile. He knew he shouldn't drink as many cups as he did, but he just couldn't seem to stop. The same was true with Nicole.

"Being bothered by a woman like you definitely has its complications," he murmured. Seeing her look of confusion, he hooked one of his long arms around her shoulder and tugged her closer. "This is one powerful complication right here..." Using his free hand, Chase softly brushed his thumb over her lower lip. "You have the sexiest mouth...do you know that?"

Nicole shook her head, which made her lips slide over the slight roughness of the fleshy pad of his thumb. The ensuing friction was incredibly arousing. She could read the need in his face, the hunger in his dark eyes. She knew what he wanted. But she wasn't ready to give it to him. Not yet.

"I don't know you well enough for this to go where I think you want it to go," she felt compelled to warn him. "I mean, we've only kissed two or three times."

"I can fix that. Here—" Chase gave her a quick teasing kiss. "That's our fourth kiss. Now for our fifth..." His lips brushed hers with heat and melting tenderness. "Something a little slower," he whispered against her mouth, tracing the curvy outline with his tempting tongue.

Nicole felt a ripple of anticipation slide up her spine. Their previous embraces had been fiery and immediate. There hadn't been this gradual buildup, this sensual dalliance. It was incredibly exciting to be able to pause and enjoy the little things. The fullness of his lower lip. The way he tasted like peppermint, only better.

"Sixth. Sexy." He was as good as his word, consuming her with his passion, appealing directly to her senses. Gone were the previously playful kisses of teasing tongue and soft nibbles. Now he focused in, intent on exploring the delicacies she had to offer: the lushness of her mouth, the sinful softness of her tongue, the smooth enamel of her teeth.

"Seventh. Sexier." It was. His mouth completely engulfed hers in an impetuous seeking of souls. Nicole responded with equal fervor. Nothing short of the need for oxygen could break them apart.

Breathless, Nicole waited for his next move. It was just as creative as his others had been.

"Eighth. Earlobes." He nibbled on the sensitive skin, growling and tugging on the fleshy lobe with his teeth. She shivered, assaulted with an entirely new battery of exhilarating sensations. Sounds. She had no idea they could be so arousing! She could not only hear him breathing, she could feel it. Feel the vibrations of his growls. It made for a delightfully unique combination.

"Ninth. Neck." He slid his mouth up and down the column of her throat, adding a flick of his tongue every now and then. He was also cupping the nape of her neck with his hand, lifting her silky hair out of his way so that his kisses could drift in that direction, as well.

The slippery movement of his lips made her giggle. She liked it. A lot.

He could tell. His smile was eminently satisfied.

"Tenth. Tongue." His or hers? Nicole hazily wondered. She soon found out. He started out with a feathery caress as he licked and lapped at her as if she were a bowl of cream and he a hungry tomcat. The curve of her collarbone, the nape of her neck, the curve of her ear.

She had no idea kissing could be this much fun! And that was before he engaged her tongue in a delicious game of hide-and-seek.

From there things got passionate again. Nicole eventually called a halt somewhere between kiss twenty and twenty-five. "That's enough," she gasped while she still had the breath and the sanity to do so.

"Know me well enough yet?" he whispered wickedly.

"I know you as well as I'm going to tonight," she retorted.

"Are you sure?"

"Positive." Things were moving too fast for her.

"Okay." He released her with a readiness that immediately made her suspicious. What was he planning next? "If that's the way you want it..."

It wasn't the way she wanted it, but it was the way she knew it had to be. She wasn't emotionally ready to make love with him. The nervousness about the wild way he made her feel was still too persistent.

To her surprise and relief, Chase didn't press her, getting up instead and tugging her to her feet, as well. "See me out."

"You know," she said as she accompanied him to the back door, "we've set a record tonight. This is the longest we've ever gone without arguing."

"So it is. Maybe this is the start of something new."

"Maybe it is," she agreed.

"Then again..."

Laughing, she put her fingers over his lips. "Don't spoil it."

His tongue darted out, stroking the ultra-sensitive skin between her fingers. Just when she was about to melt, he abruptly pulled away. "It's getting late. I've got to go."

Nicole had a hard time keeping her feet on the ground as she drifted off to bed—only to dream of Chase.

Nicole spent most of the next morning at the library in a rose-colored world of her own. She came back to earth with a bump just after lunchtime as she spotted someone lurking in the back of the stacks. There was something furtive about him that made her uneasy. As luck would have it, this was Chase's afternoon off, he was working a split shift today—morning and evening.

Nicole had almost convinced herself that she was just being overly imaginative when she saw the man take a book down from the top shelf and slip something into it. He then returned the book to its original position.

That was it! Nicole had to do something. She should call someone. But wait! The man was leaving. She hadn't even gotten a clear look at him. She should follow him. Just for a bit, just to get a better look at him.

"I'm going out for a minute," she told Michelle as she passed by the desk on her way out the library's double doors. "I'll be back shortly."

She was gone before Michelle could ask any questions.

Outside Nicole casually looked both ways down the sidewalk and across the street. There he was! Walking along the sidewalk on the park side. She crossed over. There were several pedestrians around; it was a hot and sunny day and they were out enjoying the shady relief offered by the block-long park.

Nicole followed the suspicious-looking man at a safe and discreet distance, willing him to turn a bit so she could see his face. Seeing him only from the back wasn't going to be very helpful to Chase when she told him.

The man turned the corner and was momentarily blocked from view by the tall line of lilac bushes that had given the park its name. When she got to the corner, he was gone!

Nine

Nicole looked around in dismay. There was no sign of the man she'd been trailing. In fact, there was no sign of anyone in this corner of the park. How could she have lost him so quickly? He'd only been out of sight a minute or two.

She was still pondering the question when she was abruptly grabbed from behind and yanked into the dense foliage of a group of huge bushes. A rough hand over her mouth prevented her from screaming.

Nicole was frozen with fear. The man obviously hadn't disappeared after all! He'd been hiding, knowing she was following. And he had her firmly in his grip now.

She could smell the stench of old whiskey and unwashed clothing from the body holding her so tightly. Nicole closed her eyes, willing herself to calm down.

Think. Don't panic. Escape.

"Don't even think about biting me," a familiar voice growled in her ear.

She was imagining things. She'd gone off the deep end. In her panic, she was hearing Chase's voice.

"Did you hear me?" the voice said again, turning her toward him so that she could see his face.

The eyes. Brown eyes. Sloping at the outer corners. The mouth. She'd kissed that mouth! It was Chase!

Nicole went limp with relief.

"Don't pass out on me," he growled.

She wrinkled her nose at the odoriferous aroma originating from him. He was dressed as a derelict. This close, he smelled like one, too.

Apparently satisfied that she was neither going to pass out nor scream, Chase removed his hand from her mouth and instead gripped both her arms as if he wanted to give her a good shaking. "What the hell do you think you were doing?" he demanded in a furious whisper. "You may have ruined everything, you idiot!" He angrily shook her—once, twice. "Of all the stupid, asinine things to do!"

He was glaring at her with such unconcealed resentment that Nicole wished she could sink into the ground and disappear. Humiliation rolled over her in waves. His growling voice amply expressed his feelings of rage. He sounded utterly disgusted with her.

"I saw you put something in a book," she tried to explain. "I didn't know it was you. I just saw some man. I was following you..."

"I know damn well what you were doing. Getting in the way!"

"I had no way of knowing it was you!" Nicole protested. "I was just trying to help."

"You help me any more and I could end up getting killed!"

His words hit her as powerfully as physical blows. Wounded to the quick, the pain was so intense that Nicole actually felt ill.

Chase had unknowingly made a direct hit on her Achilles' heel. Guilt. Blame. The all too familiar twin demons. He could have been killed and it would have been her fault.

Oh, God, not again. The agonizing thought rushed through her head like a hot train. *Not to be responsible again!*

Chase realized he was being harsh, but dammit—Nicole had put herself in a very dangerous position by following him the way she had. What if he *had* been some derelict placing a bet? Or a member of the gambling ring? She'd certainly have to deal with more than just anger then. Anything could have happened. While the ring had never been violent in the past, anything was possible. When you cornered a rat, it fought back. Didn't she have any idea what could have happened to her?

"No more reckless behavior or I'll lock you up personally," he informed her.

"That won't be necessary," she said, retreating behind a wall of dignity to hide her pain. *Reckless,* her mind taunted. *See what happens when you act without thinking?* "Please let me go."

Looking down at her face, Chase realized that he'd hurt her. Her green eyes were huge in her pale face. But it was their expression that concerned him. Those normally fiery emerald eyes of hers were empty. Devoid of emotion. He'd never seen her look like that.

A group of rowdy children playing nearby distracted him for a moment, and in that split second Nicole slid from his grasp and fled as if the devil himself was on her heels.

Chase let her go. He couldn't really blame her for taking off so quickly. He *had* come down pretty hard on her. But that was because she'd scared him. He'd never expected her to come trailing after him.

Now that some of his initial fear had receded, he felt a grudging respect for what she'd done. It had taken guts and quick thinking on her part to follow him so promptly. She had done it well, acting casual and keeping her distance. Most wouldn't have noticed her trailing them. But he had.

He'd been stunned. Who would have thought that a classy reserved lady like her would take on the role of super sleuth? He had to admire her spunk—and he had to examine his own reasons for getting so furious with her.

The thought of her being in danger had turned his blood cold. A woman able to warm his blood—now that was easy to label as attraction. But the fear he'd felt at the thought of Nicole in danger—that had to mean he'd gone and done it. He cared for her. He *really* cared for her. Big time. It had finally happened, just as he'd been afraid it would. Somehow he didn't find the prospect quite as daunting as he would have a few weeks ago.

He'd fallen for her. Hard.

Great. He'd not only fouled up his chance to nab one of the gambling ring's runners today, he may also have fouled up his chances with Nicole. He'd make it up to her later, Chase told himself. Meanwhile, he had work to do.

"Did you do it?" Eddie asked Leo.

"Yes. No problems," Leo assured him. "I made the scheduled pickups."

"Did that new guy show?"

"What new guy?"

"A new client. He was supposed to place his bets..." Eddie sorted through the various slips of paper he held in his hand. "Yes, here it is."

"Business seems to be picking up," Leo noted.

"Yeah. Relocating to this library was a smart move. They were getting suspicious at the last place. I could sense it. I've got a sixth sense about those things, you know."

"I read an interesting book on extrasensory perception."

"I don't want to hear about it. You read too many books, Leo. That's what's wrong with you. You need to get out and live life more, not read about it in some book."

"The line of work you have me doing gives me plenty of excitement," Leo said.

"Is that a complaint?"

"No, no," Leo quickly denied. "Merely an observation."

"Because there are plenty of people I could have hired for this job, you know. I didn't have to hire you."

"I realize that."

"If you weren't my wife's cousin . . ."

"At least you know you can trust me," Leo pointed out. "Look on the bright side."

"I'll let *you* do that. Me, I'll keep track of the money."

Nicole returned to the library and locked herself in the staff washroom, where she grabbed a bar of soap and fiercely scrubbed her hands and bare arms of the whiskey scent that clung to them. She then splashed cold water on her face and angrily ordered herself to stop shaking.

Her fingers clenched the edge of the sink as she fought back the tears. She'd been deluding herself. Chase had never cared for her at all. She'd been a dalliance, nothing more. An amusement. Until she'd gotten in his way and made a nuisance of herself. Then she'd become a hindrance.

Even worse, she could have put his life in danger. That was enough to make any man furious with her. She was furious with herself. When would she learn?

She tried telling herself that what she was feeling was residual pain left over from the tragedy with Johnny. Chase had hit her where it would hurt the most, ripping off the scab from an old wound that ran very deep. But this pain was different; fresher, more intense. This wasn't just an old wound, it was the beginning of a new one.

Nicole then tried reassuring herself that at least she'd come to her senses before things had gotten too involved between herself and Chase. Before she'd done anything else too reckless. One slipup had been enough.

That's what happened when you developed feelings for men who walked on the edge of trouble, she noted bitterly. Anything you did might knock them off. It was too damn easy for those cocky self-assured rebels to fall right off that edge and into the danger that was there, waiting below, ready to consume them and devastate you.

It took a great deal of resolve for her to leave the washroom and face her curious staff.

"Are you all right?" Michelle asked in concern. "You lit out of here so fast...and then when you came back, you looked ill."

"I'm not feeling very well," Nicole admitted with a fragile smile. "I should know better than to go racing around in this kind of heat and humidity. It would even make Michael Jordan wilt."

"I didn't know you knew anything about basketball."

"Well, I guess you learn something new every day." Just as she'd learned what Chase *really* thought of her. That very first time he'd kissed her, on her back patio, she remembered thinking he'd cavalierly treated her as if she were a pesky nuisance. She should have trusted that first impression. It had turned out to be a very accurate one.

"Are you okay?" Michelle asked again. "You still don't look right."

Nicole didn't feel right, either. But she gutsily stuck it out, refusing to give in to the dark emotions threatening to overcome her. She answered reference questions for patrons who didn't even ask them. When someone came in asking about the major events of 1972 for an anniversary party, Nicole gave the poor man more information than he really wanted to know: most popular TV shows, songs, headlines, books, Broadway shows, scientific developments, world events. Nicole covered them all, because it kept her busy and forced her to concentrate on what she was doing instead of the aching chasm inside of her.

But when she got home, the events of the day and the subsequent emotions hit her all over again. She made it inside her front door before the tears inundated her. The force of her emotions was all the stronger for her having suppressed them all afternoon.

Nicole could barely see her way upstairs to her bedroom for the tears blurring her eyes and flowing down her cheeks. Once in her room, she ripped off her clothing and went into the adjoining bathroom to take a long hot shower. There, her tears were free to mingle with the water from the shower as she stuck her head directly under the shower nozzle.

She stayed there until the warm water turned cold. By the time she'd dressed in a thin cotton gown and a matching robe, she felt all cried out, like an empty shell. Acting on a thought that had occurred to her while in the shower, Nicole made her way downstairs and checked all the locks. Just in case Chase got the notion that she needed another fiery raking over the coals.

She didn't want to see him tonight. Or tomorrow, or the next day. But she'd have no choice about that. She had to work with him, until the case was closed. But tonight was hers. And she was declaring her home to be a police-free zone.

He could damn well stay out of her life and she'd certainly stay out of his. But when she came back from the living room, she found him standing in her kitchen. She'd locked the back door, she was sure of it, but he'd gotten in anyway. He was wearing his trademark black T-shirt and the seductively holey jeans he'd worn the very first time she'd ever seen him.

"I told you," Chase murmured, "I haven't met a lock I couldn't master."

"Go away." Her voice was dripping with ice. It would have frozen most men right there and then. But Chase wasn't most men.

"We need to talk," he stated.

"*Yell,* you mean," she frostily corrected him while deliberately tightening the belt on her cotton robe. "Don't bother. You did plenty of that already."

"I was not yelling."

"Whatever you say."

Chase could see that she wasn't in a real receptive mood. Not that he'd expected her to be, after the way he'd treated her in the park earlier. But he hadn't expected her to be this remote and distant.

He only knew one way of dealing with her deep freeze tactics. And that was to evoke her passion—get her mad, get her speaking to him at least. Yelling... anything was better than this silent treatment and that lost look in her eyes.

With that idea in mind, Chase said, "What you did this afternoon was very stupid."

"You told me that already," she replied distantly.

"Well, it bears repeating."

"Consider it repeated. Please leave."

"I'm not going anywhere until we have this out."

"Fine. You stay here. *I'll* leave then." She headed for the front door before remembering she wasn't dressed to go out. Realizing her error, she veered at the last minute, intending to race up the stairs, which were conveniently located right across the foyer from the door.

Unfortunately, Chase got there before her and effectively blocked her exit by planting himself on the third step. "Don't you think you're overreacting a little here?"

That got a response from her. "Overreacting? When I was almost mugged this afternoon—by you? When I was then verbally abused—"

"I didn't verbally abuse you," Chase interrupted her, pleased to see her old fire was coming back, even if she was still madder than hell at him. "I was yelling at you."

"Two minutes ago you said you hadn't yelled at me."

"I was yelling at a whisper," he amended.

"Growling."

"I didn't want to be detected."

"You didn't want to be arrested."

"I'm a cop. I wouldn't have been arrested. I was concerned about you."

"Concerned about your case is more like it."

"The chief would kill me if anything happened to you."

So now he'd only been concerned about her because of the chief. Great. What else had she expected? "Well, neither you nor the chief will have any more cause for concern, I can assure you," she said bitterly. "I'll be a good little librarian and stay behind the desk, buried beneath my pile of books."

Her sarcasm angered him even further. "Better you do that than try to play some super sleuth. You could have been hurt!"

"We've been through this before." Her voice turned brittle. "I told you that I won't get in your way again. You have my word on it. You won't catch me getting within a mile of your precious case. I'll stay as far away as possible."

"I don't want that."

"I don't care what you want."

Chase tried another tact. "Look, I can understand why you did what you did. I realize you were only trying to be helpful. And I realize that I may have come down a little hard on you."

"A little!"

"But that was out of concern," he told her.

"Sure," she scoffed. "Concern that the chief might be upset if something happened to me."

"No, concern because *I'd* be upset if something happened to you. Damned upset." Disturbed by her accusation, Chase abandoned his sentry post on her third step to follow Nicole as she headed toward the living room. "I care about you, lady! Can't you tell that?"

Nicole turned to look at him in disbelief. "That's the way you show someone you care about them? By yelling at them?"

"Yes." He glared at her.

She glared back before looking away. "It doesn't matter."

"It damn well *does* matter." To prove his point, Chase took her in his arms.

Had he kissed her with anger or with force, Nicole would have been able to resist without difficulty. But he deviously chose tenderness instead and she was lost—lost in the wonder of his mouth caressing hers.

It was as if he were telling her without words how he felt about her. The gentleness of his touch was almost her undoing. But she didn't dare believe him. He'd fooled her before. She wasn't going to let him do it again.

She finally broke away. "No! You're not doing this to me again. You're not seducing me into forgetting my reason. Not this time."

"I hurt you," he gruffly acknowledged. "I'm sorry about that. But don't you see that I wouldn't have been that upset if I hadn't been worried about you? After I calmed down, I realized I'd been wrong to jump on you the way I did. To tell you the truth, part of me had to admire your actions. You surprised me. I wasn't expecting that kind of spontaneous behavior from you."

"Reckless behavior, you mean."

"You weren't as reckless as you could have been. You kept your distance. You stayed back—"

"I should have stayed away," Nicole interrupted him. "Completely away. From you, from everything."

"That's an unrealistic expectation for someone with your passion. You get involved. You're not the kind to sit there and take a backseat. You're not the kind to back down from a fight. After I lit into you, I expected you to fight back...sock me or something. That's why I was so surprised when you went all quiet and your green eyes got all big and wounded, as if you were a kitten I'd just kicked."

"So you're feeling guilty now, is that it? Well, forget it!" she shouted.

"I'm not feeling guilty. I want to know why you reacted the way you did. I want to understand."

"That's a first for you," she retorted.

"Damn right it is, so you'd better act on it now while you can."

"I'll pass. I made one slipup with you. That was enough. You're the kind of man who delights in walking right on the edge, always on the verge of trouble."

"There's no way you're going to convince me that you don't enjoy trouble, too—not after the way you acted today, taking off after me like that. Not to mention kissing me the way you just did."

"You make me feel reckless and I don't like it! It's no good being reckless with a man like you. Because you walk so close to the edge, that anything I do might knock you off."

"Knock me off, as in get rid of me permanently?"

Chase meant it as a joke, but Nicole's expression was tortured. "It's happened before," she whispered.

"What are you talking about?"

"The last time I was reckless, the man I loved ended up getting killed. Don't look so disbelieving. I'm telling you the truth."

Or her impression of the truth, Chase silently noted, knowing from experience that emotional impressions had a way of coloring the facts, adding shades that had never actually been there in the first place. "Just tell me what happened."

The thought of actually telling Chase about Johnny felt strange, but Nicole could see that he wasn't going anywhere until she did. So she tried to get it over with as quickly as possible. "I met him when I was in college. He was on the wild side, just like you. Loved a challenge. Not that I gave him much of one. I fell for him like a ton of bricks."

Chase wondered if pushing Nicole to tell him this had been such a good idea after all. Because the thought of her loving another guy made Chase burn inside, as if he'd eaten bad seafood and then been hit with a baseball bat. He'd experienced both of those occurrences. But he'd never had a woman make him feel this way before.

"We were together for three years." Nicole's words came out faster now. "Like I said, he was a rebel, a bit on the wild side. Nothing illegal, no drugs. It was just part of his nature to always push the envelope, as he put it. To see how far he could go. Well, one day he went too far. He was riding his motorcycle, a Harley-Davidson. He smiled at me and promised me I'd be really impressed with what he'd learned to do with it. He was showing off, just fooling around. But something went wrong." Nicole squeezed her eyes shut before opening them and keeping them fixed on the calm seascape she had hanging on her living room wall. It was easier to keep the tears at bay that way. "He crashed and died. While I watched."

"So that's it. Oh, honey..." Chase's voice wrapped her in its husky warmth. "Come here." He slowly opened his arms, inviting her into their protective sanctuary.

But Nicole held back, hesitant to expose herself once again to the kind of pain he'd already caused her. She didn't want to risk it. He'd hurt her deeply, whether he'd intended to or not.

Then she looked into his expressive brown eyes and the warmth she saw there held such promise of healing that she took one step forward...then another, before she was close enough for his strong arms to tenderly enfold her. He held her close to his heart, gently rocking her to and fro.

"Have you been feeling guilty all this time?" he murmured in her ear.

"You don't understand," she whispered in a choked voice that tore at his heart. "I could have stopped him, but I didn't and he was killed. So when you said this afternoon that I could have gotten *you* killed..."

Chase swore softly. "I was blowing off steam. A natural reaction when the woman I care about scares me half to death. I didn't mean it."

"Yes, you did."

"Well, at the time I might have meant it... I mean, I might have been angry enough to mean it... Dammit, I had no way of knowing about your background! If you'd have told me about it, I wouldn't have said what I did." Chase tilted her face up so he could see her eyes. She'd never seen him look so solemn. "I'd rather cut off my right arm than hurt you." He brushed his lips over her cheek in a series of gentle, soft kisses that spoke of remorse and tender reassurance.

Chase abandoned words in favor of showing her how he felt, letting his kisses express everything, holding nothing back. This was his way of telling her that she'd awakened a need within him that he hadn't known he had—a need to be close to her, to protect her from harm, to care for her.

Nicole cherished this new, added dimension of their embrace. Their earlier chemistry was now strengthened by an underlying foundation of emotion. She had no trouble deciphering his silent declarations. How could she when his mouth was so fluent at telling her what she needed to hear without him speaking a word? His hands were equally eloquent, caressing her with the utmost care.

His wandering lips were mapping the planes of her face with exquisite detail and when they neared the corner of her mouth, Nicole turned her head so that their lips met. Now their kiss moved beyond the preliminary stages to the next level of intimacy. It was a subtle progression, moving through layers of rich emotions: pain, healing, sharing, understanding, needing, wanting.

She'd expected a more aggressive approach, but Chase took his time wooing her. His arms were loosely clasped around her waist as he held her to him not by physical means but by emotional ones. They were linked together by ethereal chains. She moved closer, silently marveling at the ease with which her body fit into his, like matching pieces of an intricate jigsaw puzzle.

This was where she wanted to be—in his arms. Where she was meant to be. Where she *belonged*.

Nicole was overcome by an incredible feeling of acceptance. This was right. She'd never felt this way before. She knew now. She had no doubts about what she wanted.

"Not here," Nicole whispered against his mouth.

"Not here?" Chase groaned, but gamely loosened his hold on her.

"No, not here." She kept her lips near his, unable to break contact completely, even to tell him what she had to say. "Upstairs."

"Upstairs?" he repeated, pulling away from the temptation of her mouth to stare down into her upturned face. The certainty he saw there made him catch his breath.

Nicole smiled and nodded. "Upstairs." She brushed his mouth with hers.

This time his groan was filled with anticipation as he deepened the kiss. Neither one of them wanted to break the physical contact, so—amidst her laughter and his growls of approval—they continued their series of kisses as they made their way across her living room to the stairway.

Once there, Nicole creatively decided to back her way up the steps. That way she was facing him so that her lips didn't have to leave his for longer than a second at a time.

At the top of the steps, Chase took matters into his own hands by sweeping her up into his arms and growling, "Which way?"

Nicole didn't waste what little breath she had on speaking. Instead, keeping one arm linked around his neck, she pointed to the door at the end of the hall. He moved so quickly that she barely had time to get accustomed to having him carry her before they'd reached her room.

She'd left the bedside light on and had turned down the bed earlier. The aqua-and-white striped sheets made her antique bed look wonderfully inviting.

Chase set her on the crisp sheets with care, handling her as if she were his most prized and precious possession. He'd never displayed such open tenderness toward her before. As she leaned back against the pillows, Nicole briefly reflected on the roller coaster ride her emotions had been through. It was amazing to think of the pain she'd felt in this very room not two hours ago. Now here she was, filled with excitement and anticipation for what was yet to come.

Sitting beside her, Chase lifted his hand to push a strand of her silky blond hair away from her face. Once that was done, he continued touching her, his fingers slowly trailing down the side of her face until they reached the corner of her mouth. Then his thumb took over, brushing her parted lips, thrilling her with the sheer simplicity of his touch.

Nicole couldn't get over the effect he had on her. It was as if they'd known each other before, and yet had never felt this way with anyone else. As if their hearts recognized and welcomed what their minds had fought—that they were meant to be together.

Cupping her face between his hands, Chase leaned over until his mouth was almost touching her. Eyes closed, Nicole waited with bated breath for the feel of his lips on hers. Slowly, deliberately, Chase rebuilt the ardent fires, starting with a gentle kiss to the corners of her mouth.

His lips moved sensuously and oh-so-persuasively over hers while his hand leisurely cruised down the length of her arm. The memory of his touch lingered on long after he'd moved on, so that by the time he reached her hand, her entire arm was alive with sensual energy, nerve endings humming.

As he slid his fingers between hers, Chase could feel them trembling. "Nervous?" he murmured in a deep velvety voice that was as seductive as his touch.

"Charmed," she breathlessly corrected him.

"Good." Raising her hand to his mouth, he flicked the tip of his tongue over her knuckles. "So am I. But don't take my word for it." He placed her hand on his chest, inviting her to explore him as he was exploring her. "Check it out for yourself."

He expected her to be tentative. He thought he'd have to reassure her. But Nicole caught him by surprise once again, whisking his T-shirt over his head and tossing it over the curved foot of the bed. Then she tugged him down to her, shifting so that he was flat on the bed. He groaned with delight as she hovered over him, plying him with little kisses from the tip of his shoulder to the dip of his navel.

Meanwhile her hands were busy, sliding up his thigh and darting inside one of the more provocative locations of a ripped hole in his jeans.

"Do you know what you're doing?" Chase inquired unsteadily.

"Seducing you. I hope I'm doing it right!" Nicole shot him a mischievous look while moving her hand upward.

He closed his eyes and smiled. "Oh, honey, you're doing it *just* right..."

When her touch got too intimate for him to bear without completely loosing control, Chase threaded his fingers through her hair, dragging her lips back to his.

He'd just begun unwrapping her robe and kissing the newly exposed creaminess of her skin when he suddenly sat up, startling her. "Oh, no!"

"What's the matter?" she asked him in a breathless voice.

Chase ran his hand through his tousled hair, hair she had mussed with her combing fingers, and pressed the heel of his hand against his forehead in the manner of a man badly besieged. "I wasn't expecting ... I didn't come here planning to do this ... so I didn't bring any protection with me."

Nicole found his uncharacteristically jumbled delivery to be quite touching.

"Good thing I've got some, then," she murmured, reaching over for the drawer in the nightstand and withdrawing a box. She had been forced to drive twenty miles away to a hugely impersonal super mall before she had felt comfortable buying them, fairly certain that she would not run into someone she knew. She'd bought them after that night Chase had bestowed kisses number five through twenty-five upon her.

Still she hadn't looked at the box very carefully before buying them and it was only when she'd gotten home that she realized these were the technicolor variety. "They're blue," she apologetically warned him.

"Blue?"

"At least they don't glow in the dark!" she said defensively.

"I had no idea you were this well versed on the selection of condoms available today."

"I'm not. The truth is that I grabbed the first box I came to."

He looked at the box and then at her. "Blue, huh?"

"Afraid so."

"Could be interesting," he said.

"I'm sure it will be," she demurely agreed.

"Okay, now that we've got that matter settled, where were we...?"

"Right here." She pointed to her collarbone.

"Actually I think it was closer to here..." His lips moved closer to the swell of her breast.

Turning so that she was beneath him, Chase set to work on the buttons running from the scooped neckline of her gown to the ruffled hemline. She marveled at his dexterity and delighted in his creativity as he slowly undid each one, celebrating his accomplishment with one kiss for every pearly button successfully slipped through its buttonhole.

By the time he'd completed his self-assigned task, Nicole was basking in the glow of his meticulous attention. Taking his time, Chase peeled away the delicate cotton to reveal the equally delicate treasures beneath, unwrapping her as if she were an erotic present. Before she could slide her arms free of the armholes of her gown, he lowered his head and placed his mouth directly over the rosy tip of her lush breast.

Burning up inside, Nicole arched upward, startled by the incredible sensations coursing through her. Not wanting her other breast to feel left out, Chase moved his hand to cup and claim her fevered skin. Holding her in the palm of his hand, he used his thumb to skim over the creamy terrain.

When Nicole thought the pleasure too great to be borne, he switched sides, moving his mouth to her left breast where she thought he must surely be able to feel the erratic beat of her heart.

His caressing fingers moved southward, grazing the inward curve of her waist, then the outward flair of her hips before settling on the one place still aching for his attention. The silky tap pants she wore allowed him free access as he ministered to her needs, both satisfying and provoking them.

He made her feel like she was soaring right into the sun. At this rate she'd disintegrate. She didn't care! She didn't want him to stop.

Things happened very quickly after that. Nicole hazily realized that somehow the rest of his clothing had disappeared. So had her tap pants.

Chase briefly rolled away from her to put on the protection she'd provided for him and then he was back with her. He came to her slowly, timing his movements to her ability to accept him. She welcomed him eagerly, bending her knees and tugging him to her.

Rocking against her, Chase smiled down at her, watching the rapt expression on her flushed face with primitive satisfaction. When she involuntarily tightened around him, he groaned at the exquisite torture. And when she moved against him, he almost lost what little control he had left.

Nicole slid her hands down the slickness of his back, holding on to him as her entire being pulsed with such exquisite pleasure that she couldn't speak, couldn't think. All she could do was feel—and feel—and *feel!*

Ten

"We've done it now," Nicole languidly murmured some time later.

"We certainly have." The warm male shoulder on which she was resting her head resonated with the husky baritone pitch of his voice. "Not regretting it, are you?" Chase asked.

"I don't know yet," she answered truthfully. "There's a lot I don't know...about you."

"What do you want to know?"

She shifted her hand on his chest until she found the reassuring beat of his heart. "Everything."

"Oh, that's real specific."

"Do you realize that I don't even know where you live? You show up at the library dressed as Alvin, you show up at my back door—mysteriously, out of the blue—kiss me and then disappear again."

"I'm not disappearing now."

"Not yet." She looked up at him, noting the new perspective she got from this angle. His chin and jaw looked rock-hard and particularly stubborn, while the curve of his mouth was sensually appealing.

"Oh, ye of little faith," Chase murmured.

Shifting so that he could see her more clearly, he smiled down at her. And that's when it hit Nicole that she wasn't merely unbelievably, irresistibly attracted to Chase—she loved him with all her heart. She didn't even know his home address or phone number, but she loved him.

It should have been a frightening discovery, but it wasn't. While she might not have certain facts about Chase at her fingertips, she had the man himself beneath her fingertips. And she'd learned a lot about him over the course of their time together—not just tonight, but over the past few weeks.

She knew he had his own way of doing things and that he wasn't easily swayed. She knew he was capable of great tenderness and compassion. And she knew she loved him. Her mind may have waited until now to acknowledge that fact, but in her heart of hearts she'd known for a while.

"Why are you looking at me that way?" Chase asked her.

Because I just realized that I love you. And I'm trying to figure out if your saying you care for me means you love me, too. Aloud, she said, "No reason."

"Trying to figure me out?" he astutely guessed, threading his fingers through her hair in an absent-minded way that she found surprisingly soothing.

"Something like that."

"I was born thirty-four years ago on the south side of Chicago."

"And?" she prompted.

"And—" he spread out his arms in a violà gesture "—here I am!"

"Come on." She trailed her index finger over his bare chest. "You know about my romantic past, but I don't know anything about yours. Have you ever been married? Engaged?"

"No. Yes."

"You were engaged?" The news caused Nicole to momentarily stop her teasing caress. The twist of jealousy she'd experienced when he'd flirted with the giggling teenagers at the library was nothing compared to what she was experiencing now. "What happened?"

"We had a disagreement over my work. She wanted me to go into politics. I didn't agree, but that didn't matter to her. She had her rich daddy try and pull a few strings to move me off the force. I found out about it."

"She must not have known you very well to think *you'd* ever make it as a politician."

"Should I be insulted by that comment?" Chase inquired dryly.

Nicole propped herself up on one elbow to stare down at him. "No. Don't get me wrong. I'm not saying you couldn't *play* the role of a politician and act the part if you wanted to—it's certainly been done before," she added with a grin. "But you're much too independent to make it in the world of politics. Too rebellious. Too everything."

"I'll take that as a compliment. And you're right, she didn't know me very well."

"But then you don't really let anyone get to know you, do you?" she noted quietly. "I wonder why that is."

"I like to keep you guessing—keeps you on your toes."

She'd expected him to sidestep her question, but thought it worth a try anyway. "I didn't realize you wanted me on my toes," she retorted.

"I want you any way I can have you."

Just want her? Or love her? Would she ever really find out? Because she couldn't help wondering if Chase didn't use his wickedly flirtatious ways as a means of keeping people at bay, the same way she used her responsible and classy image to protect herself. There was no doubt about it, Chase was a difficult man to get to know. You'd have to reach your own conclusions about him, because he wouldn't tell you much—not without pulling it out of him.

"I still know nothing about your life outside of your work," Nicole pointed out.

"I don't have a life aside from my work."

She thought it was a telling reply. "Even if you don't have a life, you must live somewhere."

"I have an apartment. I sleep there. I'm not sure I ever really *lived* there."

Another enlightening admission, she noted. "What made you decide to go into police work?"

"I liked dressing up."

She socked his arm. "I'm serious."

"So am I. Of course, first and foremost I wanted to save the world," he modestly claimed. "But aside from that, I also have this flair for the dramatic."

"I had noticed that," she noted dryly.

"So my dad said, 'Son, with a talent like yours you can either be a cop or an actor.' I decided to be a cop. Steadier work. I think I was five at the time."

While Chase might kid about it, she was learning that he did that about the things that were the most important to him. "Your dad's a drama teacher, right?" she asked, remembering he had mentioned that earlier.

"That's right."

"My dad was a teacher, too," Nicole told him. "American history. He's retired now."

"That surprises me," Chase said.

"What, that my dad's retired?"

"No, that he was a teacher. With your classy attitude I would have thought your dad would have been a banker or something. I had you pegged as being born with a silver spoon in your mouth."

"Hardly. My background is very middle class."

"Your foreground is very upper class," he noted wickedly, brushing the curve of her breast with his fingertip. He was in the process of lifting her arm out of his way when he noticed the angry-looking scratch there. He frowned. "When did this happen? Just now?"

"No. Earlier today. The bushes..." Her voice trailed off because she was reluctant to discuss what had happened in the park earlier that day.

"I'm sorry." Chase kissed the faint redness on her skin. "I should have realized that you might see me and get suspicious."

"It wasn't your fault," she earnestly assured him, wanting to erase the haunted look in his eyes. "You played that role very convincingly, I must say. I had no idea it was you."

"Thank you." His smile was wry. "I like to think I'm pretty good at what I do."

"You're *very* good at what you do—on and off duty." Hoping to lighten the mood, she teasingly added, "I just have one question...was that a gun you were carrying or..."

"Or was I just glad to see you?" Chase completed the infamous Mae West line for her. "The answer to both questions is yes."

The fact that he'd been armed subdued her earlier attempt at flippancy. She didn't like to think about the danger his carrying a gun implied. "I didn't mean to ruin things..."

He put his fingers over her lips. "I should have set up some kind of contingency plan for you to put into place in case you saw something suspicious when I wasn't there. I did tell you to call Chief Straud as I recall, however," he added with a stern look.

"I wouldn't have been able to tell him anything except that a strange-looking man had put something in a book.

And then he'd have come and disrupted your sting anyway. That's what it was, right? A sting to catch this ring."

"That's what it was supposed to be, but it backfired."

"Because of me."

"I have to take equal blame," Chase told her. "I overreacted. I could have just given you the slip. Instead I yanked you into the bushes and read you the riot act, injuring this beautiful arm in the process." He kissed the wounded limb, moving his way up and around from her wrist to the tip of her shoulder.

"Just don't do it again," she said breathlessly.

"Don't do *it* again?" he said, deliberately misunderstanding her. "Was making love with me so disappointing for you?"

"Your head is swollen enough without me answering that question," Nicole retorted.

"My head isn't the only thing . . ."

She clamped her hand over his mouth. "Don't say it. You've got a naughty mouth, Detective Ellis. Seems to me I should do something about that."

"What did you have in mind?" he mumbled around her constraining fingers.

"Forcing you to tell me your past. Start talking, mister."

"Did I ever tell you about the summer I spent placing road signs?" Chase inquired. "I put up those signs you see on the side of the road. You know the ones. The warning signs." He traced her jawline with a teasing finger. "The danger signs." His voice was darkly promising as he curved his hand around the back of her neck. Then he trailed his fingers down the gentle valley of her spine.

"For example, right here—" Chase shifted his hand until it was touching the outer swell of her breast "—right here should be a sign that says Curve Ahead."

His hand slid to her waist. "Road Narrows should go here."

"And here..." His hand lowered, touching her very intimately, very seductively. "Here would be Yield."

As his fingers continued to gently probe her ultra-sensitive warmth, he wickedly murmured, "Slippery When Wet." The richness of his touch was skillfully provocative, a sensual fingerplay that progressed to its ultimate denouement. His butterfly-soft caresses soon had Nicole gasping his name as a series of erotic tremors quivered within her.

Rolling away, he quickly took care of their protection before returning. "And finally—" he whispered, looking at her with heated tenderness "—Merging Ahead."

He came to her with one gliding thrust, filling her with his throbbing strength. The erotically delicate clenching of her muscles as she peaked almost undid him.

But Chase wanted more. He wanted her completely wild. Wanton. Out of control.

So he held himself still, waiting until her climax was complete. Then he began to move again, rhythmically stroking her with his body. He could tell by her gasp of pleasure and the passionate darkness of her eyes that it wouldn't be long before she'd peak again.

He felt the pleasurable pain of her fingernails biting into his back as he partially withdrew and then rushed forward again. Faster, faster. The tempo matching the pulse throbbing deep within her and within him.

And then he felt it. The convulsive little shudders beckoning him onwards. Flash. Heat. Energy. Explosions.

He could conquer the world. He was invincible. She made him feel that way. His shout of triumph was matched by her sultry smile.

As he held her in his arms afterward, basking in the moment, she lazily murmured, "I'll never view road signs the same way again."

Chase's last thought before falling asleep was that he'd never view *anything* the same way again—not after having fallen for Nicole.

"You're in an exceptionally good mood today," Anna commented to Nicole the next morning at work.

"I'm in a good mood every day," Nicole countered.

"Not this good. I tell you that sixty-five sixth-graders are coming in looking for books on the Civil War and you're not even upset that the teacher didn't notify us ahead of time."

"I am upset," Nicole said. "But at least we found out in time to save a few books and put them on reserve for use here. We'll refer the rest of the people to other area libraries. I've written a letter to the teacher involved, reminding her of the procedures we've set up with the schools about advance notice for a school project requiring extensive use of a particular body of work."

Body... Nicole's thoughts drifted, as they'd been apt to do all morning, to Chase and their incredible night together. At the moment he was out of sight, reading the shelves in the stacks. She remembered his provocative comment about reading *her* shelves. She remembered the way he felt in her arms, the way he kissed her, the way...

"...So do you think that would be appropriate?" Nicole vaguely heard Anna ask her.

She forced her attention back onto Anna. "I'm sorry. What did you say?"

"I asked you if you thought it would be appropriate for me to contact the parents of the third-grader who's been causing trouble. It's pretty clear that his parents are using the library as a baby-sitting facility. They just stash him here. He comes here straight from school and often has to stay until well after seven before someone comes to get him."

"Definitely contact his parents," Nicole agreed. "Contact the school, as well. Much as we might like to offer the library as a safe haven, we can't be a baby-sitting service. The insurance liabilities alone..."

"What's this about insurance liabilities?" Mr. Query demanded, seemingly from out of no place. "Is someone suing us?"

"Not at all," Nicole assured him. "We were merely discussing the reasons why the library can't be responsible for unsupervised children for hours at a time, day after day."

"That's one point on which we agree," Mr. Query noted approvingly.

"Still, sometimes it's hard for working mothers to find sitters," Michelle bravely pointed out.

"I know it is," Nicole said. "And I feel for women in that kind of situation. But there is help available from the county social services department."

Casting a frosty look Michelle's way, Mr. Query regally informed Nicole, "I need to speak to you. Is there someplace private..."

"...Where can we talk?" Nicole completed for him, knowing what he was going to say, since he never varied it. She led the way to her office.

"I don't like the way your staff is answering back," he said. "They're getting ideas above their station."

Ideas above their station? Nicole thought in amazement. He sounded like something right out of Dickens! "It is still a free country. Last time I checked no one had canceled the first amendment rights to free speech."

"I'm not talking about free speech, I'm talking about insubordination. Caused by lenient management."

Nicole had to relax her clenched jaw before she was able to speak. "Was that what you came here to talk to me about?"

"No. Actually I came to discuss my nephew, the one working here as a page."

"Bruce? What about him?"

"I understand you're still having him shelve books."

"That is what he was hired to do."

"Yes, but he's much too smart to be doing that. I thought he could be doing more with the computers here. He's very clever with them," Mr. Query stated.

"I'm sure he is. And if we need any additional help in that area, I'll keep him in mind."

"He's going to be studying for final exams soon . . ."

"And?"

"And I'd like him to be able to do some studying while he's here at the library."

While Bruce was supposed to be *working* at the library, Mr. Query meant. Apparently it was okay for her to have lenient management where his nephew was concerned, Nicole silently fumed.

"If he's shelved all the books, and there's absolutely nothing left for him to do, then of course we'd let him study for a few minutes during his break," Nicole assured him in such a pleasant voice that Mr. Query never suspected a thing. Of course, Bruce never *did* shelve all the books, he was very slow for all his intelligence, so Nicole wasn't actually promising a thing.

"Good. I'm glad we got that settled, then."

"No problem," Nicole said with a grin, rather pleased with the way she'd handled the situation.

After he'd left, Michelle came up to Nicole and apologized. "I hope I didn't say anything out of line."

"Don't worry about it."

Things got very hectic after that, with more people than usual filling the library on a Friday afternoon. Mr. Kedzie stopped by, requesting that Nicole order "that new book about the collapse of western civilization."

"Sure you wouldn't like to read something a little... lighter?" Nicole inquired.

"What's the point?" Mr. Kedzie gloomily inquired.

"Whatever makes you happy." Nicole was in such a glorious mood today that she wanted everyone to share it.

"Happy?" Mr. Kedzie snorted. "I haven't been happy since before the Great Depression. Which reminds me, did that book on the Depression I ordered interlibrary loan come in yet?"

"Not yet. We'll call you when it does."

Oak Heights' doomsayer had barely left when Mrs. McGillicutty requested Nicole's assistance, looking for photographs of famous strippers of the thirties and forties. "I'm thinking of writing my autobiography. I was an exotic dancer myself for a brief time," the older woman confessed. "By the way, how's that nice young man doing? The new librarian? I was hoping he'd help me today."

"He's busy," Nicole told her. Chase had told her that he needed to leave for a few hours that afternoon.

"He looks after his mother, did he tell you that? So hard to find young people who respect their mothers these days, don't you think?"

"Alvin is definitely one of a kind," Nicole agreed. So was Chase, she thought to herself. Even his name made her smile. It suited him perfectly. He was always on the go— even when he was standing still, his thoughts were racing...and racy, judging from the few heated looks he'd slid her way earlier when no one else was looking.

"You should try some ostrich feathers, my dear," Mrs. McGillicutty suggested.

Nicole blinked. "I beg your pardon?"

"For the man, whoever he is, that put that dreamy look on your face. You should try one of those big feathery fans. Let me know if you'd like me to teach you any special moves."

"I'll do that, Mrs. McGillicutty."

Once she was done with the continually surprising older woman, Nicole helped a young woman wanting career information, a gentleman needing to check state statutes regarding the legality of his firing, and a frazzled mother looking for a book on hyperactivity in children. During one of Nicole's frequent forays into the reference room, she ran into Leo.

"You look busy," Leo quietly noted, in deference to their surroundings.

Nicole nodded her agreement.

"I won't bother you then," Leo said. "I just wanted to make sure everything was doing okay here."

"Everything's fine," she replied. "Just hectic."

"Is that new librarian in today?" Leo casually inquired. "I haven't met him yet."

"No, he's not here at the moment."

"Too bad. Well, I really must be going." Leo hurried away, moving faster than Nicole could ever remember seeing him move before.

When Nicole got home later that evening, she couldn't wait to talk to Chase. To her delight, she found him waiting for her in her kitchen. As he swept her into his arms and kissed her, Nicole found herself thinking that she could get used to this...very easily indeed!

Then she remembered what she had to ask him. "How did the sting operation go this afternoon?" she inquired excitedly.

"What sting operation?" Chase countered.

"At the library."

He frowned. "What are you talking about?"

"I saw you there late this afternoon in that seedy character disguise of yours, taking something out a book. I stayed completely out of the way, just like you said."

"I wasn't at the library this afternoon. I told you I had some things to do, remember?"

"Of course I remember," she said huffily, a bit irritated by his tone of voice—the one that implied she was a simple-minded child. "When I saw you, I thought that this sting operation was the thing you had to do."

"I was following some leads I had elsewhere." Chase had some contacts out on the street and he was checking with them regarding more details about this gambling ring and how it operated. He couldn't believe what he was hearing. Judging from the ring's bumbling maneuvering he was surprised they hadn't been caught long before this. "Tell me exactly what you saw."

"Not much. I only saw the man from the back. Since I thought it was you, I deliberately stayed away so I wouldn't bother you."

Chase swore under his breath. This case was really turning out to be one wild-goose chase after another. While he might be a rebel in some regards, where his work was concerned Chase did not like complete bedlam. Normally he had a better handle on things. He wondered if his feelings for Nicole were making him lose his edge with this case. He should have caught these guys long before now, especially considering how bumbling they were supposed to be. Apparently they'd just had a hell of a lot of dumb luck.

"All right—" Chase pulled a small notebook from his back pocket "—I want you to tell me everything you remember. How tall was the guy?"

"I don't know."

"Come on, Nicole!" he said impatiently. "Taller than I am, or shorter?"

"About your height. That's one of the reasons I thought it was you."

"Build?"

"Average."

"Hair color?"

"Dark."

"You never saw his face?"

"Obviously not," she retorted. "Or I would have known it wasn't you."

"Anything unusual about him? Did you notice the way he walked, for example. Any jewelry? A watch?"

"No. I'm sorry. I only saw him briefly."

Chase flipped the notebook closed with a frustrated oath. "I can't believe they got away from me twice! I can tell you one thing, it's not going to happen again."

"No problems?" Eddie asked Leo when they met.

"No." Leo slid into the front seat of Eddie's sleek car and then handed him the slips he'd collected. "Except for this beard itching me. And these awful clothes." Leo grimaced. "Why did I have to wear a disguise this time, Eddie? I never have before. And why did I have to show up at the library undisguised first?"

"Because I saw something like this on *Kojak* once. Or was it *Columbo?* One of those cop shows. Anyway I decided it would be a very effective way to cover our tracks."

"You think someone is on to us?" Leo asked in dismay.

"Not on to us, no. I have reason to believe that others may be jealous of our good fortune and my brilliance in devising this scheme," Eddie carefully stated, thinking of the phone calls he'd been avoiding lately. "Nothing for you to worry about."

"Well, if you're sure..." Leo paused. "About this scheme, Eddie. I've been reading a few books—"

"I already told you," Eddie interrupted him. "You read too much."

"These books were about gambling. And the various procedures that are used."

"Planning on placing a bet yourself, are you?" Eddie inquired mockingly.

"No. But it was interesting to learn how the bets are recorded. This guy listed the whole thing step-by-step. Bettors have a phone number and they call into a bank of phones, where the fronts takes their bets. Then those bets are forwarded to the back, who has two phones. One phone is to receive calls from the fronts. The other phone is always kept open to relay information to the head of the ring and he's the only one who knows the number of that phone. Bettors seemed to use a lot of pay phones. No one mentioned using a library, Eddie."

"That's because it's my own system," Eddie bragged. "One I developed. And it's why I'm where I am, and the others aren't."

"And where exactly are we?" Leo asked.

"Sitting pretty," Eddie confidently assured him. "Sitting very pretty."

"This is a completely decadent idea," Nicole noted as she leaned back against the slick warmth of Chase's bare chest. They were both sitting in the large Victorian claw-footed bathtub in her bathroom. Jasmine-scented candles, over twenty of them, provided the romantic lighting while the lyrically seductive music of Rimsky-Korsakov's *Schéhérazade* provided the rest of the haremlike atmosphere.

"Totally decadent," Chase murmured. "Aren't you glad I thought of it?"

"The candles and the music were *my* idea," she reminded him.

"Creative touches," he agreed, creatively touching her with his soapy hands.

"Mmm." She shifted against him. "You make a very comfortable chair, do you know that?"

"Somehow that's not the image I was aiming for," he retorted dryly. "I must be doing something wrong here."

"This is my favorite part."

"I haven't done anything yet."

"I meant, the music."

"Oh, right. By all means let's appreciate the music. Let's see . . . how was I taught to do that . . . Oh, yes . . . by combining art and rhythm," he murmured, using his seductive fingers to sketch his way through the bubbles adorning her breasts. "That's what my seventh grade teacher told me. Picture the music . . . feel it . . . mmm, yes . . ." He brushed his thumb over one roseate tip peeking through the bubbles. Then he drew a swirling design on the creamy underside of her breast. "This definitely increases the appreciation. Don't you agree?"

"It has definite possibilities," she murmured huskily. "Too soon for me to make a decision."

"Take your time," he told her. "No hurry."

And indeed his hands were slow and skillful as he leisurely continued caressing her, seemingly fascinated with the contours of her body. The more intimate his touch, the more the passion between them grew. Turning her head, she kissed him, her tongue dueling with his. The darting movements were very erotic and she wanted more.

Nicole shifted, attempting to move so that she was facing him, and ending up banging her knee in the process. "Why are we doing this?" she laughingly asked. "There's a perfectly good bed right in the other . . . oh!" Her eyes widened and her lips parted with her breathy expression of delight as she came into intimate contact with his fully aroused body.

"Still wonder why?" he inquired devilishly.

She shook her head, unable to speak for the hungry ache throbbing deep within her. Despite the number of times they'd made love, Chase still had the ability to make her want him with a swiftness that should have embarrassed her, but didn't. When he set her away from him and stood up, she didn't look away. Instead she boldly watched the droplets of water sliding down his incredible body as he turned and grabbed for the box of condoms on the table beside the tub.

Water splashed over the side of the tub as moments later he hurriedly sank down into the water and tugged her back to him. The music played on, building in crescendo, setting the stage. Their kiss reflected the heightened state of their arousal. The intimate thrust and retreat of his tongue was a provocative prelude of what was yet to come.

Nicole was ready for him. She wanted him with her, within her. Now! Reaching down through the bubbly water, she cupped him in her hand and led him to her. Once they were joined together, she slid her legs around his hips, locking her ankles behind him. Her actions elevated their pleasure to yet another plateau. It felt so good she didn't want it to end.

She'd never considered Chase to be a patient man, but she discovered he could be infinitely patient when it suited him. And to her delight, it suited him at the moment. Suited her, too, as they slowly rocked together in an erotic water ballet—extending and prolonging the sensual spiral. The experience was sinfully decadent and luxurious.

Nicole kept her eyes open as long as possible, savoring the opportunity to watch Chase's face as she moved, tightening around him. She loved the way his eyes darkened. The flickering candlelight made him look diabolically handsome, his face all angles and shadows.

She'd never thought of herself as being a sensual woman, but now she knew better. Feeling like a wanton hedonist, she sank into the pleasure . . . drowning in the seemingly bottomless pool of sexual delight.

Ripples of ecstasy consumed her not just once, but three times as she clung to him, her face hidden in the warmth of his shoulder. Each time she was lifted to a higher level of bliss, she gasped his name.

When Chase finally found his own release, she felt the shudder rock his body before her mind became a blank as she gave herself over to the sweet euphoria they'd so lovingly created. Occasional aftershocks continued to quiver through her as she held him in her arms.

They weren't able to speak in complete sentences until they'd both dried off and lay sprawled in utter satisfaction on her bed. Even then, they were too emotionally spent to speak of any but mundane things.

"Nice bed," Chase laconically noted.

"Mmm," she lazily agreed. "It's a sleigh bed. I got it out at the Kane County Flea Market."

"You got this bed at a flea market?"

"Not just the bed, but that rocking chair over there, as well. And the carved wooden sandpiper on my dresser."

Chase shifted his leg, bumping it against hers. There was a comfortable familiarity in his actions that pleased Nicole. She liked having him in her bed. It felt so right.

"Last flea market I went to sold hubcaps and other junk no one wanted," Chase noted.

She propped herself up on one elbow so that she could look at him while speaking to him. "Kane County's flea market is one of a kind. Haven't you ever been out there?"

Chase shook his head, enjoying the view as the top sheet slipped, revealing her bare breasts. She wasn't aware of the risqué situation yet, and he wasn't about to tell her. She really was the most incredible woman—part sensual woman, part excited little girl.

"They say it's the largest flea market in the world," she continued. "It's the first weekend of every month, come rain or shine, sleet or snow. Anna and I have been out there in all of the above, we usually go a couple of times each year. We often run into Leo when we do."

Chase frowned. "Who's Leo? Some other smooth collegiate type like that male librarian you went out with?"

"You sound almost jealous."

"I am almost jealous. *Almost.* So who is this Leo?"

"One of our library patrons. He's an inventor and has a special interest in the old electronics stuff they have at the flea market. We should go out there sometime. You and I."

"Why's that?" he absently asked, wanting to show her how inventive *he* could be.

"Because since I've met you, we've only seen each other here or at the library." She deliberately omitted mentioning the time he'd hauled her into the lilac bushes at the park. "We've never really gone anywhere."

"Never gone anywhere? Not ten minutes ago we left this planet entirely!" He watched the flush color her cheeks. "I don't believe it! You can still blush after what we just shared?"

She socked his arm. "I'm serious."

"So am I. Or I will be in another half hour. You've worn me out, woman."

"Poor baby," she crooned.

Chase tickled her for her impertinence. "The library is closed the Sunday before Memorial Day as well as Memorial Day, right?" he asked.

Nicole nodded.

"Great. I've got a day off coming. Where would you like to go? It would have to be someplace where no one would see us together," he added.

Nicole nodded her agreement. She didn't need reminding that in order to maintain his cover, he couldn't be seen leaving the house with her. She certainly didn't want to do anything else to endanger the investigation, or Chase's safety. "How about going downtown? I haven't been to the city in ages. We could make a day of it."

"Maybe even make a day and a night of it."

"Maybe. If you're not too worn out," she impudently added.

"Oh, I don't think you'll have to worry about that."

"No?"

"No. Let me show you...."

They'd made arrangements to rendezvous in St. Charles, at the parking lot of the Piano Factory Outlet Stores. Nicole had waffled over what to wear before deciding on her present outfit, a two-piece dress. The navy blue, double-breasted, short-sleeved, V-neck jacket topped a chiffon knife-pleated white skirt for a jaunty yet elegant look. She was waiting for Chase when he pulled up in a black Camaro.

"Need a ride, honey?" he drawled out his open car window, ogling her outrageously.

"It isn't wise to accept rides from strangers," an elderly woman standing beside Nicole cautioned her.

"It's okay. I know him," she told the woman. But the concerned advice-giver had been right about one thing: this wasn't wise. *Nothing* Nicole was doing with Chase was wise. But it was incredibly fun. Unbelievably satisfying. Deliciously daring.

Nicole got in the car.

Eleven

Chase and Nicole spent the hour-long drive downtown enjoying the freedom of sharing: looks, childhood memories. And comparing: favorite pizza joints, fast food hamburger places. The latter had them in a heated argument.

"I'm telling you, the secret is in the onions," Chase categorically declared in defense of the hamburgers that he'd grown up with on the city's south side. "It's the onions.. and the buns."

"I'm not getting into a discussion of buns with you," she haughtily returned. "Although yours are pretty good looking, Detective," she wickedly added, sliding her hand down his back and finagling her fingers an inch or two beneath the waistband of his black slacks.

"Watch it . . ." he warned her.

"I'd like to!"

"I fear I've become a bad influence on you," he solemnly stated.

"Is that a complaint?"

"Your timing could use some improvement."

"Spoilsport."

"We could just turn the car around and head for the nearest motel."

"No, that's okay." Nicole prudently kept her hands to herself after that. "You haven't told me exactly where we're going downtown."

"I thought we'd start out with a little brunch..."

"Sounds good."

"On top of the John—"

"A unique place for a brunch, I'm sure!" she noted with a saucy grin.

"The John Hancock building."

"Really? At the restaurant up there?"

"No, on top of the TV antennas," Chase retorted teasingly. "Of course at the restaurant."

"Isn't it expensive?"

"You're worth it."

The view was also worth it, Nicole decided as she looked out the window before following the maître d' to their reserved table. She hadn't been on top of the Hancock Center since she'd been a teenager, and then it had been a visit to the observatory one floor lower.

Thankfully, it was a beautifully clear day. The lake, dotted with tiny sailboats, shimmered in the sunshine while toy cars crawled in the Sunday traffic along Lake Shore Drive's sweeping curve. Nicole was momentarily stymied by the hundreds of brightly colored specks on Oak Street Beach, until she figured out that they were sunbathers. Lots of them.

From this high up, nothing looked real. In fact, the scenery reminded her of the model train set her brother had had as a kid and the made-to-scale world her father had constructed on a sheet of plywood. Only the world she was viewing now was even smaller.

"We're taller than the Eiffel Tower by forty-three meters," Chase informed her as they sat. "Just thought you'd want to know that."

"Been checking out the pamphlet file, have you?" she inquired.

"How do you know I haven't memorized millions of those kinds of trivial facts?"

"In all your spare time, you mean?"

"Exactly."

"Because you've been reading shelves, dealing with computer skills, checking out books, and checking out criminals in your spare time."

"Not to mention making love to you," he added.

"Not to mention that," she agreed with a meaningful look at their approaching waiter.

After filling up at the impressive spread laid out for their brunching delight, Nicole suggested walking for a bit along Michigan Avenue. They window-shopped at some of the expensive stores along the Magnificent Mile. Then they hailed a cab to take them the few blocks south to the Art Institute of Chicago.

"We could have walked faster than getting there this way," Chase grumbled as they stopped at their third red light in a row.

"These shoes weren't made for that much walking," she countered, wiggling her ankle meaningfully as she displayed her spectator pumps for his perusal, knowing he'd appreciate the view of her legs. "What mileage they do have in them I want to save for the museum. It's been ages since I've visited the Monets and Van Goghs."

"You visit *paintings?* Sounds kind of strange, Nicole."

"You'll see what I mean," she promised.

When they got out of the cab, Chase was still shaking his head at her comment. "Look!" He teasingly grabbed her by the arm and showed her some paintings hanging in the display window of a nearby art gallery. "Here are some paintings! Want to visit them?"

She watched his overzealous performance with amused suspicion. "You wouldn't by any chance be trying to avoid going into the art museum, now would you?"

"What makes you ask that?"

"The panicked look in your eyes when I told you I wanted to visit the museum."

"I'm here, aren't I?"

"That's right. *You're* here. But the *museum's* across the street."

"Fine. We'll cross the street." Holding her hand, he rushed her across Michigan Avenue on the tail end of a Don't Walk signal.

"That was illegal," she reprimanded him.

"I like living dangerously."

"Then you'll be brave enough to come inside the museum," she countered, nudging him toward the steps flanked by the famous pair of massive bronze lions.

"Did I ever tell you about the time I climbed on those lions during my fifth-grade field trip?" Chase inquired.

"No." She tugged him up another step. "And you're not telling me now, either."

"It's nothing personal that I have against art," he assured her with an earnestness she recognized as being a complete put-on. "I like art. It's just that I have some reservations about those dumb names they use. Like Dodoism."

"You mean Dadaism. And we'll stay away from those pieces if they traumatize you so much. Don't tell me you're afraid of a little culture?" she challenged him.

Before Chase could reply, their teasing was abruptly interrupted as a young man ran past them followed by cries of "Stop him! He stole my purse!"

The shouts were coming from an elderly lady.

The young man who had just raced past them had the woman's purse on his arm.

Nicole didn't even have time to blink before Chase took off.

"Call the police!" Chase yelled over his shoulder as he began pursuing the young man, dodging startled on-lookers and pedestrians.

It happened so fast that Nicole couldn't move. Stunned, she watched in horror as, seconds later, Chase doggedly followed the purse-snatcher—straight into the heavy traffic on Michigan Avenue!

Nicole could see the car heading straight for him. The horrifying vision became a freeze-frame nightmare. Suddenly everything went from fast forward to slow motion. She heard the dismayed gasps of the surrounding crowd. She opened her mouth to cry out—a warning, a protest—but no sound came. Her throat was frozen. So was her heart.

Paralyzed with fear, Nicole stood there helpless to prevent history from repeating itself as the air was filled with the scream of squealing brakes. It was a scream echoed deep in her soul. A scream of anguish.

For Nicole, the world tilted and changed again in the blink of an eye as Chase miraculously eluded the car only to almost get hit by a cab coming in the other direction. Had he been saved from the jaws of death only to be tossed right back again? she wondered in despair. He was running the gauntlet of disaster and she was sure that any second now he was going to get hit as he wove in and out of oncoming traffic—across six lanes of traffic.

There were so many close calls that Nicole lost track of them. It was only when he'd safely reached the other side of the street that she remembered his shouted instructions to her. He'd run around the corner and was out of sight by the time Nicole had pulled herself together enough to move on legs that were shaking so much her knees were knocking.

The police were duly called by the security people right inside the museum entrance. Knowing that her legs weren't going to support her much longer and seeing that there were no empty seats on the crowded foyer, Nicole returned outside in search of someplace quiet to sit down and collect herself—if that was possible. At the moment she felt so shattered that she wasn't sure she'd be able to find all the pieces of herself, let alone put them back together again in any kind of order.

A cement bench nearby provided a welcome respite. It didn't matter that it wasn't the cleanest bench in the world. It was solid and didn't move. That was all she wanted at the moment. To hang on to something solid.

Nicole sank onto it, shaking with fear as flashes of Johnny's fatal accident came back to her. Seeing him die right in front of her. Moments ago she thought she'd be seeing the same thing happen to Chase. It had happened so fast; one instant she and Chase were smiling and laughing together, the next instant danger appeared. The same thing had happened with Johnny—laughter before sudden death.

She sat there, tensely fingering the pleats in her skirt. She had no idea how much time elapsed before a Chicago police car pulled up at the curb in front of her. Her heart stopped. Were they coming to tell her that Chase was dead?

A man was getting out of the back of the squad car. A man with dark hair. Chase? Was it Chase? A teasing lake breeze blew around the corner of the museum behind her, blowing her hair into her eyes. Impatiently shoving the strands aside, she saw that it was indeed Chase. She started breathing again.

Spotting her, he flashed her a jaunty thumbs-up sign before turning to speak to the uniformed police officer who'd joined him.

Nicole didn't even realize that the woman whose purse had been stolen was sitting on the next bench over until Chase and the other police officer approached the older woman. She heard their conversation as if from a great distance.

"Where's my purse?" the woman demanded stridently.

"Here." Chase handed it to her.

"It's all dirty. But everything seems to be in here. Thank you," she added grudgingly.

Nicole couldn't believe it. Chase risked his life for what? A stupid purse? A woman who didn't even fully appreciate what he'd done? Didn't she realize that Chase had almost been killed by that car? Was her precious purse worth it?

Nicole was so incensed that she only heard every other word after that. "... Come to the station... give a statement... give you a ride..."

The uniformed police officer escorted the woman to the waiting squad car, which then sped away.

"Well, that was exciting!" Chase noted cheerfully, sitting next to Nicole and jubilantly placing an arm around her stiff shoulders. "I caught the guy. I'm not as out of shape as I thought I'd be after spending so much time in the library. Ready to visit those paintings of yours now?"

"I'm not feeling very well," she said in a strained voice. "I'd like to leave."

"But we haven't gone inside the museum yet."

"I'd rather go home now."

"You do look a little pale," Chase belatedly noted. "You weren't scared, were you? There was no need for you to be worried."

"Of course there wasn't. Just because you practically threw yourself in front of a speeding car, that's no reason to be upset," she sarcastically replied. "Let alone the fact that that kid could have had a weapon for all you knew. Did you think about that before you took off like a bat out of hell?"

"I'm carrying a weapon, too," Chase replied.

Ah, yes. The gun. The one she kept trying to forget about, because it represented the dangerous life-and-death edge of his job.

Chase then made the mistake of saying, "I knew what I was doing."

"So did Johnny when he crashed his motorbike," Nicole bitterly replied. "That's exactly what he told me. 'I know what I'm doing,' he said."

"There's no similarity," Chase angrily denied.

"Isn't there? I don't want to talk about it," she said, her voice cracking. She knew if they kept arguing, she'd make a fool of herself by crying right there in the middle of the sidewalk. And she didn't want to do that.

"Fine. Let's go."

As Nicole approached her front door, she painfully reflected on what a difference a few hours could make. When she'd left the house earlier that morning, she'd been excited about her upcoming day with Chase. She'd even brought along a sexy scrap of a nightie in her large purse, in case they'd decided to spend the night downtown.

Instead here she was, a basket case. She'd driven her car home from the parking lot by putting herself on automatic pilot. She didn't know where Chase was. During their return drive from the city, she and Chase hadn't spoken more than five words to each other. Silence had reigned. Nicole had been a prisoner of her own anguished thoughts.

Chase could have been killed. She'd come so close to losing him, too damn close! Too damn close to never being able to hold him again, never being able to kiss him again, to laugh with him, to see his wicked smile, his endearing grin.

She supposed she shouldn't have been surprised to see him in her living room—waiting for her. He'd obviously exceeded the speed limits in that Camaro of his to get there before she did. He was smiling that endearing grin of his and he looked so unconcerned that it infuriated Nicole.

She walked over and socked his arm, *hard*. "Don't ever do that to me again!" she sobbed. "I thought you were going to be killed. Don't ever do that to me again! Don't ever do that to me again!" She kept repeating those words until he stopped them with a kiss. The moment his lips touched hers, their passion flared out of control.

Nicole's relief that Chase was alive and unharmed provided the heat, her passionate love for him provided the tinder. She went up in flames. And so did he.

Everything else was forgotten in their need to be together. Clothing was a nuisance and they got rid of their own and each other's with quick dispatch, her fingers bumping into his as they both worked on undoing the stubborn catch of her bra. Their discarded clothes ended up in a heap on the floor and they ended up in a heap on her living room couch.

Outside, a flash of lightning heralded the arrival of an approaching storm. Inside, a jolt of heat heralded his arrival within her body as they came together in a turbulent storm of need. There had barely been time for him to rip open a foil packet and don its contents. There had barely been time for her to toss her panties out of the way.

It didn't matter. This was all that mattered. This moment. The passion and the pleasure drowning out the fear. Each thrust of his body erasing the pain. Each convulsive ripple of ecstasy blocking out the torment.

But afterward, for the first time ever, Nicole felt unsatisfied. Not physically, but emotionally. Because the same insurmountable problem was still there. Their lovemaking, incredible as it had been, hadn't made the fear disappear. It had merely been an interval, like that between the increasing lightning and thunder. During that interval, things were quiet. Then another lightning bolt shot out of the sky and the storm raged on.

Nicole had an emotional storm of her own to contend with. She loved Chase. She'd loved Johnny. It didn't seem to stop them from taking chances. From daring death. Risking the odds. She didn't want to gamble anymore. She couldn't cope. The stakes were too high. She closed her eyes as if that would enable her to shut out the pain.

She felt Chase move away from her, heard the rustle of him gathering his clothes, followed by the sharp slam of the bathroom door. While he was gone, she took the opportunity to run upstairs and pull on her robe. Chase was waiting for her, buttoning up his shirt, when she returned downstairs.

"Are we going to talk about this or are you going to just keep giving me the cold shoulder routine?" he inquired.

"It's not a routine!" she flared, resenting his ability to remain so calm. "You're the one with the drama training. Not me. I don't find it that easy to hide my emotions."

"Or lack of them."

"What's that supposed to mean?"

"It means that one minute you were with me every step of the way while we're making love and the next . . . it was as if you'd turned off the switch. You backed away."

"I backed away because I didn't want to get hurt."

"Was I that rough?" he asked in a low, taut voice.

"Not physically hurt me. There are other ways of causing me pain! This is tearing me apart. Don't you see? I can't keep this up. I can't keep pretending that I'm not hurting when I am. And it's going to keep happening, because that's just the way you are."

"You're still angry with me about what happened in front of the Art Institute."

"Angry doesn't even come close!" Her voice shook with the force of her emotions. "You knew about Johnny, but you still ran out and acted recklessly."

"Stop comparing me to him! I'm a cop. Not a cocky teenager showing off on my motorcycle."

"No," she shot back. "You've got to prove your machismo with your gun instead!"

"What do you expect me to do? Just stand back and allow a crime to occur?"

"I should know better than to expect anything," Nicole said. "There's no talking to you men."

"Quite the contrary," Chase retorted. "It's *women* who are completely unreasonable! You keep comparing me to your precious Johnny, when the truth is that you're more like my ex-fiancée than I'm like him. Maybe I should do a little comparing of my own. Just like you, she couldn't accept me for what I am. She wanted to change me, too."

"You could use some changing!" Nicole retorted, hurt that he was comparing her to *that* woman. "You go off and flirt with death and come swaggering back, proud of how easily you got off, at how easily you won . . . this time. But what about next time? I can't live like that."

"Nobody asked you to."

Nicole felt as if he'd slapped her. "You're absolutely right. Nobody asked me to." Chase had never made any mention of them sharing a future together, she bitterly reminded herself. She'd been a fool to think that his silence had been caused by his difficulty to express his emotions. Apparently there hadn't been any emotions for him to express. Unlike her, he'd never said the words *I love you* because he'd never felt the emotions. "And even if you did," she proudly added, "I'd say no."

"I guess that says it all, then." She'd never heard his voice go so cold. And his face could have been carved in stone, so austere was it. "I'm outta here."

Chase still had the presence of mind to leave by the back way. Nothing was going to take his mind off work, she noted in despair. When it came to his cover he knew how to be careful. But when it came to his own safety and well-being, then he seemed to enjoy being reckless.

She wondered if he'd missed that element of risk and danger during his tenure at the library. This job must seem tame to him. No doubt that's why he hadn't wanted it in the first place. It was too boring for him. Too sedate. And so was she.

Nicole angrily wiped away the tears. She wasn't going to do this again. She was not going to cry herself sick over him. She was going to forget all the reasons she'd fallen in love with him in the first place. There weren't that many reasons, were there?

So he was patient when he showed people how to use the library's computers, teasing them into learning, making them forget their insecurities. The way he'd made her forget hers. Temporarily.

So he took the time to talk to the lonely senior citizens who wanted to chat while they checked out their books. And he'd also taken the time to chat with Michelle's unruly son, George, who had miraculously settled down some since then. Plus he'd convinced Dayton to let her tutor him, and the older man's lessons were progressing well.

Okay, so the man had a few good points. That didn't change the fact that he was a trouble-making rebel who had a hazardous addiction to danger. He loved trouble. He didn't love her. She remembered how jubilant he'd been after his near brush with death, how delighted with himself he'd been. It was as if he'd gotten a thrill from the danger, gotten a kick out of the entire experience. The only kick she'd received had been the one to her stomach when she'd feared for his life.

She couldn't do this again. It had been hard enough the last time. But the thought of losing Chase was more than she could bear.

You've lost him anyway, a mocking voice inside her head told her. You sent him away.

"I never really had him in the first place," she whispered. "He was only on loan."

So what had she learned from this experience? Nicole asked herself.

A lot of little things: that when she stood before Chase, she could rest her head on his shoulder without having to stand on tiptoe; that when she wore heels, his lips reached her forehead; that bathtubs were meant for more than just bathing.

And one big one. That men like him weren't meant to be loved. Not by women like her.

When Nicole was upset, she baked. She baked a *lot* that night. It seemed better than just sitting in bed, crying. Been There, Did That, as her T-shirt said.

So she spent her time whipping up batch after batch of frosted brownies in the microwave. She'd promised to bring something to the town's huge Memorial Day Picnic at Lilac Park the next afternoon. Although the day dawned clear and sunny, Nicole knew the holiday would only be memorable to her because of the pain she felt. Exhaustion had dulled her emotions enough for her to go through the motions.

She'd taken a quick shower and gotten dressed in a pair of khaki walking shorts and a maroon polo shirt. She'd even managed to show up at the picnic on time when she would much rather have stayed home, in bed, with the covers pulled over head.

But she had obligations to fulfill, responsibilities to meet. As head librarian, her presence was required at this village function. So here she was. And there was Anna, manning the bake sale booth.

"Here. I brought a few brownies," Nicole told Anna.

"I'd say that was an understatement," Anna replied as she took the two huge containers that Nicole handed over. "Looks like you've been busy."

"Keeps me off the streets," Nicole said with a brightness that was one hundred percent artificial.

Anna wasn't fooled for a minute. "You look about as good as I feel," the normally cheerful Anna solemnly noted.

"What's the matter?"

"I've been seeing this man," Anna confessed. "Well, not exactly *seeing* him. Bumping into him here and there. Anyway, we're complete opposites. He's much more of an introvert. Not someone you'd ever think that I'd be attracted to."

"Does this mystery man have a name?" Nicole asked.

Looking over Nicole's shoulder, Anna appeared flustered. "I'd rather not say anything more right now. Not until my thoughts are a little clearer."

"Okay."

"Oh, I almost forgot. The police chief was looking for you."

"He was?" Nicole tried not to look alarmed. "Did he happen to mention why?"

"Maybe he was just wondering when you'd be bringing these great tasting brownies. I know you gave me the recipe but they never turn out this good when I make them."

"I use imported cocoa," Nicole absently noted while scanning the crowd in search of Chief Straud. And Chase. Or Alvin.

"Uh, you haven't seen Alvin here this afternoon, have you?" Nicole casually inquired.

"No," Anna replied. "Were you expecting him?"

"Not really." But then Chase always did the unexpected. Like breaking her heart. Or had that been so unexpected after all? Given his personality and hers, maybe it had just been inevitable.

Thinking about him was too painful. Murmuring a farewell to Anna, Nicole moved on before she started brooding too much.

She tried to mingle, hoping some of the buoyant atmosphere would rub off on her. Instead it merely made her feel even more isolated and lonely. It seemed as if everyone else was having a glorious time. She'd never seen so many smiling faces and chins dripping with ice cream or—in the case of those in the watermelon-eating contest—watermelon juice.

Red, white, and blue banners were festooned from tree to tree, adding to the park's patriotically festive appearance. The lilac blossoms were just about gone from the bushes now. They'd lasted about as long as she and Chase had. Couldn't take the heat. Neither could she. She couldn't take the emotional heat of being put through the wringer each time she saw Chase, wondering what reckless stunt he'd pull next.

She turned forlorn eyes toward the far corner of the park where Chase had angrily yanked her into the bushes. She should have kept her distance after that. But then she'd never have known what it was like to be with Chase, to have made love with him, to have touched the stars with him.

Better to have loved and lost than never to have loved at all, right? Baloney!

"Ah, there you are, Nicole," Chief Straud said with a hearty smile. "I've been looking for you. I wanted to check in with you, see how you were doing."

"Well, here I am," she said irritably. "You can stop worrying about me now."

"Everything okay?"

"Dandy. Just dandy."

"Funny, that's exactly what our mutual friend said when I asked him how things were going," the chief stated.

"When did you talk to him?"

"About an hour ago. He didn't sound like he was in a very good mood."

"Well, I'm in a wonderful mood," Nicole declared with a toss of her head. All that got her was a strand of hair in her eye. Figures. She blinked and nonchalantly slid the rest of her hair behind one ear before it could do any more damage. "Couldn't be better."

"Who are you trying to convince? Yourself or me?"

"I'd better not answer that on the grounds that I might incriminate myself," she replied.

"Want me to arrest him?"

Nicole gave the chief a startled look. "Arrest who?"

"The man who put those dark circles under your eyes and that hollow look on your face."

"Normally I'd say yes, but the guy has connections in the department."

"That's what I was afraid of." The chief sighed. "I feel responsible. If I hadn't introduced the two of you..." He sighed again, more heftily this time. "Is there anything I can do?"

"No. Thanks for the offer."

"If it makes you feel any better, I think the man in question is just as miserable as you are," the chief said.

Somehow, Nicole doubted that.

* * *

"Anything new to report?" Eddie asked in between bites of a chili dog. In an attempt to fit in with the patriotic theme of the park picnic, he was wearing an electric blue T-shirt under his dark red silk suit.

"She was talking to the police chief," Leo replied in a distracted tone of voice.

Eddie frowned. "I hope she's not suspicious. I don't have to tell you what that would mean, do I?"

"Trouble, right?"

"Right."

"Don't you worry, Eddie," Leo reassured him. "I'll take care of Nicole. Everything will be fine. You'll see. Just fine."

The sun was setting by the time Nicole wearily let herself in the front door of her house. The brownies had been a hit. She was glad something had gone well. Because she felt totally depressed.

The cool rush of an air-conditioned breeze hit her flushed face like a sweet balm. Normally she would have plopped down on the couch and not moved for an hour or so. But she and Chase had made love on that couch. She didn't know if she'd ever be able to sit on it again.

That was the problem, one of many. Memories of him were everywhere. She stepped into the kitchen, where it was easy to imagine him sitting at her table the way he had that first night he'd invaded her home. How many times had she seen him at that table, egging her on, teasing her, tempting her, surprising her, delighting her?

While Chase's presence was still there, in reality the kitchen was empty. The garbage did need taking out, however, she noted with a wrinkle of her nose. She'd meant to do that before she'd left for the picnic, but had forgotten.

After unlocking the back door, Nicole went outside, where the purple haze of twilight was settling in. She still hadn't gotten that back patio light replaced, she noted with a despondent sigh. She'd only taken a few steps when she caught a slight movement out of the corner of her eye.

"Chase?" she murmured, squinting in the shadowy light.

"No, it's Leo."

Leo? What on earth was he doing here? Her phone number and address were unlisted, so how had he even found out where she lived? Before she could ask him any of those questions, Leo came toward her and frantically said, "I've got to speak to you, Nicole! It's urgent!"

"Calm down and come on inside."

"No. Not here." He looked around as if the bushes might have ears. "At my house. It's not far."

"But, Leo..."

"I won't take no for an answer!" was Leo's ominous warning before taking Nicole by the arm and hustling her away.

Twelve

———

"So, you want to tell me what's going on or are you just going to sit there glaring at your beer all night?" Carlos demanded as Chase and he sat in the corner of Nick's Tavern.

"Nothing's going on," Chase replied.

"I tell you that the case we'd been breaking our butts on for the past six months is finally being wrapped up and you just sit there and mope?"

"I was on that case with you for five of those six months," Chase reminded him. "Ever think maybe I'm just upset about not being in on the grand finale?"

Carlos looked concerned. "Is that really what's bothering you?"

Chase felt uncomfortable lying to his partner. For some reason he suddenly remembered Nicole telling him, *You never let anyone get to know you, do you Chase? I wonder why that is?* Chase was beginning to wonder about that himself. Why was it so hard for him to drop his quips and just tell the truth? Could it be that he'd gotten so used to

acting, to covering things up, that he'd almost forgotten how
to open up? Maybe it was time he tried it.

"No," he admitted slowly. "That's not really what's
bothering me. It's..."

"Yes?" Carlos prompted. "Go ahead. Spit it out."

"It's a woman, okay?" Chase ground out.

To Chase's disgust, Carlos had the nerve to actually
chuckle. "This has got to be a first." Carlos chuckled again,
even more merrily this time. "Normally *you're* the one giving women fits, not the other way around."

"Forget it," Chase retorted, telling himself that *this* was
why he didn't open up more often. Who wanted their private life and innermost emotions ridiculed? Not him! "Just
forget I said a thing."

"Hey, no need to get touchy," Carlos complained.

"You try being stuck in some backwater town library!
We're talking about a place that shuts down their two traffic lights on Main Street at 11:00 p.m. every night."

"Forget the town. What about the woman?"

"You know what she said?" Chase demanded, as if he
couldn't hold it inside any longer.

"No. Why don't you tell me?"

"She said I had trouble relating to people. Can you believe that? Me? Having trouble relating to people? I get
along great with everybody."

"What did she mean by relating?" Carlos asked.

"I don't know." Chase shifted uncomfortably. "Opening up, talking to people about my feelings." Seeing the look
in his partner's eyes, Chase said, "Okay, so I don't do that.
What guy does? Give me a break!"

"Just how serious have things gotten between you two?"

"We had a fight," Chase said, sidestepping Carlos's
question.

"So what's new? From what you told me before, I got the
impression you two fought a lot."

"We do. I mean, we did. But this time it was different. This time... I've fallen for her, buddy," Chase announced with dramatic gloom.

"Have you told her? Because if you did, and you told her the way you told me, I don't think you'd get any brownie points."

Chase glared. "What's that supposed to mean?"

"It means that when you tell a lady you care about her, you shouldn't make it sound as if you're announcing the end of the world, or declaring you have a terminal illness. Sound a little more pleased about it."

"I'm *not* pleased about it," Chase retorted. "Not at the moment, anyway. Why do I do this to myself? I find these classy women who want to change me, tie me down."

"Is that what this lady wanted to do?"

"She can't handle the fact that I have a dangerous job."

Carlos nodded understandingly. "It's something we run into a lot as cops. An occupational hazard, huh? If you're in trouble, the first thing you do is call a cop, but hey, you don't want to get involved with him. You just want him to put his life on the line everyday and get the job done."

"She's been burned before."

"By a cop?"

"No. A guy she loved before." The thought of her loving Johnny still bothered him. It wasn't so much the fact that she'd loved before as it was the way she glorified the guy's memory. How was he supposed to compete with a ghost? "He died right in front of her. Wiped out on his motorcycle. And when she saw me running after a suspect, dodging the oncoming cars on Michigan Avenue, she thought I was going to die, too."

"Slow down a minute. What suspect?" Carlos demanded.

Chase briefly told him about the purse-snatcher he'd caught and Nicole's subsequent reaction to his heroics.

"So where do you go from here?" Carlos asked him.

"I don't know," Chase said. "I just don't know."

By the time Chase reached Nicole's house, he still didn't know what he was going to do. He wasn't even sure why he was there. When he'd left Nick's Tavern it had seemed like a good idea—stopping by to talk to Nicole about the argument they'd had. He just found it hard to leave things as they were.

He went around back, the way he always did. But something wasn't right. The backdoor was wide open. Chase checked to make sure his weapon was easily accessible as he cautiously moved forward.

It was probably nothing, he told himself. Nicole was probably right inside the kitchen about to come out onto the patio. But his instincts were on full alert. And he hadn't been a cop for over ten years without learning to trust his instincts in these matters.

There was no sign of Nicole in the kitchen. Or in the rest of the house. Chase checked every inch, top to bottom. The lights were on in the kitchen, her purse was on the table by the front door, her car still in the driveway.

He went back out onto the patio and saw something shining in the dark. Moving closer, he realized it was a plastic garbage bag with its contents partially spilled out, as if someone had dropped it in a hurry.

Damn! Getting out his high-intensity pocket flashlight, Chase efficiently scanned the area for further clues. There, to one side, were scuffled footprints, two pairs.

Chase knew in his gut. Knew that someone had taken her. Someone from the gambling ring. There was no other logical explanation for her disappearance.

He swore softly, trying to hold back the cold fear, mentally kicking himself for underestimating the potential for danger. He'd had these guys pegged as penny-ante shysters. Somehow they must have gotten wind of his investigation.

They felt threatened and that made them as unpredictable as any cornered animal.

Chase wasted no time in calling the chief and reporting what he'd found. "There's no concrete proof," Chase added. "Some signs of a scuffle, but the footprints aren't definitive. No other sign of a struggle. Maybe she just went to visit a neighbor or something."

"It's the *or something* I'm worried about," Chief Straud retorted.

"Me, too," Chase curtly agreed.

"What do you plan on doing next?"

"Checking in with a few informants, leaning on them for information. I'll get back to you when I learn something." *When* not *if.* Chase was determined to get the information he needed, and at the moment he wasn't real picky about *how* he got it. Not when Nicole's safety was in the balance. "I'll check in again in an hour."

The bar Chase walked into a few minutes later made Nick's Tavern look like the Hilton. "Ah, Joey, just the guy I was looking for," Chase noted as he sat down next to a weasely looking man sitting alone at a bar stool.

"Whadever it is, I had nudin' to do wid it," Joey stated.

"I need a name, Joey, and I need it fast." Chase leaned closer, intimidating the other man by his very presence, since he topped the guy by a good seven inches. "See, this is personal," Chase growled. "So I might be inclined to cut a few corners. You must have heard that I've never been one to follow the rules much anyway," he added with such a dangerous glint in his eyes that Joey squirmed uneasily.

"Whadaya want?" Joey demanded.

"You know that gambling operation we talked about before?"

Joey nodded.

"I want a name. Now!" Chase barked.

"I tol' ya, I don' know..."

"You wouldn't want me to haul you down to headquarters for questioning, now would you?" Chase inquired, moving even closer with an unmistakable threat. "Then your boss might get a little antsy, wondering what beans you were spilling. Or I could just shake it out of you right here. I told you. This is personal now. I'm officially off duty."

"Keep yer voice down, wudya?" Joey whispered with a panicked look around him. "All I know is dat da guy is called Leo the Shrimp. Dat's all I got, I swear," he blabbed, seeing the murderous look on Chase's face. "I hear he's local, some kind of inventor."

Something clicked in Chase's mind. He and Nicole, laying in bed together, with her telling him about the flea market and a guy named Leo... a library patron she met out there. An inventor. It was worth a shot. How many local guys named Leo who were inventors could there be?

"One more thin'," Joey added as Chase released him. "Word out on da streets is dat another guy's in'erested in dis ring. Name's Fritz Demato. Heard of him?"

Chase had heard of him all right. While still a two-bit hood, Fritz Demato had a record of violence and was considered to be dangerous.

"Fritz don' like folks buttin' in on 'is turf. I hear he's not in a good mood, if ya get my meanin'."

Chase got his meaning. Next thing he was going to get was Leo's address and check this thing out. He could only hope his hunch was right and pray he wouldn't be too late. If anything happened to Nicole, he didn't know what he'd do.

"I'm sorry about this," Leo said as he handed Nicole a cup of tea. "I only had lemon, no sugar."

"That's okay." Nicole set the tea onto the end table at her elbow. "So you dragged me all the way over here..."

"To talk about Anna," Leo concluded. "That's right."

"I had no idea the two of you were seeing each other."

"We've sort of been bumping into each other."

Nicole remembered Anna using the same expression earlier at the picnic. "Why couldn't we discuss this at my house?" Nicole asked.

"She might come over."

"Unlikely."

"Okay, I admit it. I panicked," Leo said sheepishly. "When I overheard her talking to you earlier today at the picnic, it seemed like she was confiding in you."

That would explain Anna's strangely flustered expression after looking over Nicole's shoulder. Her friend must have seen Leo.

"I'm in love with her," Leo declared. "I don't know where to go from here." He paused before going on. "I need you advice. What do you think I should do? I confess I—"

"I think you should both freeze!" Eddie ordered from the hallway. "Don't move!" He emphasized his order by waving a gun at them.

"Eddie, what are you doing?" Leo asked in dismay.

"Protecting my hide! I heard you. You were about to confess and squeal to the little librarian here, who happens to be like this—" Eddie crossed his fingers, almost dropping the gun in the process "—with a certain undercover cop."

"What are you talking about?" Leo said.

"They're on to us," Eddie announced. "And you double-crossed me." He glared at Leo.

"I didn't do anything," Leo denied.

"Can it!" Eddie declared. "*I'm* doing the talking here."

Nicole observed these goings-on as if they were happening to someone else. But there was something startlingly real about the gun Eddie was waving around. She'd never been held at gunpoint before. She didn't like it.

Eddie tossed a length of clothesline, complete with a wooden clothespin or two, at Leo. "Here. Tie her up."

Leo hesitated. "But Eddie—"

"Do it." Eddie waved the gun again. "Now!"

"You're making a big mistake," Leo maintained.

"Not another word. You—" He aimed the gun directly at Nicole, who'd been eyeing the nearest exit. "Don't even think about trying to make a run for it. Hurry up, Leo. I haven't got all day. Or would you rather I shot you and tied her up myself?"

"I'm hurrying, I'm hurrying. I'm sorry," Leo murmured regretfully to Nicole as he tied her to the straight-backed chair she'd been sitting in.

"Why would you get involved with something like this, Leo?" Nicole asked him.

"For the money. For my inventions."

"So you broke the law? Oh, Leo..."

"Don't sound so surprised," Eddie said. "You knew what was going on, Ms. Head Librarian. That's why you were speaking to the police chief earlier today. You told me you'd take care of her, Leo."

"She didn't know anything," Leo replied. "We were talking about something else."

"Sure you were," Eddie murmured mockingly. "Shut up and finish tying her up."

Nicole couldn't believe this was happening to her. Why, oh why, hadn't she fought against going with Leo? Had he really told his cousin that he'd "take care of her"? Gentle Leo? Gentle Leo, who was clearly involved up to his eyeballs in an illegal betting operation, she reminded herself.

"Okay, you're next," Eddie told Leo. "Sit on that chair next to her. And not one false move or I'll shoot you," Eddie warned as he tied Leo up with efficient speed.

"I'm sorry about this," Leo repeated to Nicole as Eddie tied the final knot. He looked at her with sad puppy dog eyes. "I never meant for you to get in trouble, Nicole."

"I can't believe you'd let yourself get involved in something like this," Nicole said.

"It's not that dishonorable a profession. Gambling has been around since prehistoric times," Leo said. "Thousands of years ago the Greeks used to wager stakes on chariot races. I read about it in a book—"

"Fascinating, I'm sure," Eddie interrupted. "I think, given the current situation, that you two would do better to be concerned about staying alive than tracing the history of gambling."

Leo returned his attention to Eddie, who nervously wiped the sweat gathering above his upper lip. "You've got it all wrong, Eddie. When you walked in I was asking her for advice on my love life. I was about to confess that I don't know much about women. We weren't talking about you or anything about the work at all."

"Your love life? Yeah, right," Eddie retorted. "Tell me another one. You don't *have* a love life, Leo."

"No, really," Leo said sincerely. "I'm telling the truth. I swear it. Tell him, Nicole."

"He's in love with the children's librarian," Nicole said.

Leo frowned at her. "I didn't mean you had to tell him who the woman in question actually was," Leo chastised her.

"I think it's a little late to be worrying about discretion here, Leo," she retorted.

"I agree," Eddie inserted. "How come you never told me you had a thing for this woman? I would have given you advice. Why go to her?" Eddie waved the gun at Nicole, and the way his hands were shaking didn't exactly reassure her.

"I'm sorry," Leo humbly replied. "I thought you'd make fun of me."

Eddie looked at the two of them, clearly undecided about his next move.

"Untie us, Eddie," Leo pleaded. "Please! Think what your wife's going to say. You know I'm her favorite cousin."

Nicole watched as Eddie wavered. He lowered the gun to the table and was coming toward them when someone else burst into the room.

Nicole was hoping against hope that it would be Chase coming to her rescue. Unfortunately it was some guy in the brightest pink suit she'd ever seen. What interested her even more at this point was the gun he was holding. It was twice as big as Eddie's.

"Don't move!" the newcomer snarled.

One look at Eddie's face told her that this was not a good development, if she'd had any doubts about that.

"Mr. D-Demato. . ." Eddie stuttered.

"I been looking for you, Eddie. You didn't return my calls so I decided to tail you myself. You been cuttin' into my business, friend, and that doesn't please me."

"I've tried to stay out of your way—"

"You haven't tried hard enough. No one crowds Fritz Demato!" Having made that proclamation, the newcomer punched Eddie, knocking him to the floor. Standing over him, Fritz added, "Besides, what kind of a bookie uses a library? We have a reputation to maintain, Eddie."

Had Nicole been a fly on the wall, she might have been amused by the Keystone Kops element of the current goings-on. Being tied up prevented her from fully appreciating the humor in the situation, however. So Nicole kept surreptitiously working on loosening the binding around her wrists. Her older brother had practiced his Boy Scout knots by tying her up. If she could just remember how she got loose . . .

"And you. . ." Fritz Demato leaned toward Leo menacingly. "I hear you used to work for this jerk." Fritz punctuated his comment by jerking his thumb down toward a dazed Eddie, who was still sprawled on Leo's carpet. "Well, you've got a new boss now," Fritz told Leo. "Me. You got a problem with that?"

"No, boss. No problem at all, Mr. Demato, sir," Leo hurriedly said.

"Good. And call me Fritz," he suggested while untying Leo. "Now use this same rope to tie him up." Fritz pointed to a still groggy Eddie.

Eddie, realizing that Leo had changed allegiance, was furious. "Leo, you traitor! I knew I should never have hired you!" he yelled at Leo as he efficiently tied him up. "My wife's cousin... and you turn on me like this? Whatever happened to family loyalty? What about all the things I've done for you? What about...?" Leo took the silk handkerchief out of Eddie's breast pocket and stuck it in Eddie's mouth to keep him quiet.

"This gun isn't even loaded," Fritz noted in disgust, before sticking Eddie's gun in the waistband of his expensive hand-tailored silk slacks. "Mine is," he told Leo. "So keep that in mind."

"Yes, sir."

"Fritz. Call me Fritz."

"Yes, Fritz."

"Okay, now here's the plan. I left my car outside, parked on the street. It's the black Caddy. Here are the keys." He tossed them to Leo. "You go out and start the car. Consider this to be a test. If you try anything, you'll fail this test and then I'll be forced to shoot these two. After that, I'll track you down the same way I tracked your cousin down. Have I made myself clear?"

Leo gulped and nodded.

As far as bad guys went, Nicole decided she preferred Eddie over Fritz.

Fritz smiled a reptilian smile. "Good. Then go get my car and bring it into the driveway, under that sheltering evergreen that's out there. And don't gun the engine." Fritz added. "But be fast about it. We'll need to get these two out of here in a hurry."

Chase saw Leo come out of the house. He'd seen enough during his brief glimpse through the back window to know that Nicole was tied up. He'd called the chief from the bar. He'd gotten the backup he'd wanted. But this part of the job was his. He had insisted on it.

He didn't want some rookie with an itchy trigger finger storming the place. Chase didn't trust this job to anyone but himself. So he waited, hidden from view by the overgrown bushes and evergreens surrounding the rickety Victorian house. He waited until just the right moment, then he nailed Leo, grabbing him by the collar and hauling him up against the rough bark of an oak tree.

"Tell me exactly what's going on inside," Chase growled.

"Who are you?" Leo croaked. "Another rival bookie?"

Chase flashed his badge in front of Leo's bulging eyes. "I'm a cop. And that's my woman you've grabbed."

"I've never *grabbed* any woman in my entire life," Leo said in an offended whisper. "Oh, I see. You weren't speaking literally..." When Chase impatiently shook him, Leo gasped. "You must mean Nicole. She's inside."

"Is she okay?"

"She's tied up." Leo croaked as Chase's hold on him tightened yet again. "But otherwise she's fine."

"She better stay that way," Chase warned him. "Tell me exactly what's going on."

Leo did, as quickly as he could, since Chase's grip was threatening to cut off his air supply. Chase somehow managed to make sense out of Leo's garbled narration of events.

"How badly do you want to stay out of jail?" Chase asked Leo.

"Very badly," Leo quickly replied. "I've discovered that I'm not really cut out for the criminal life. I'm not very good at it. And I feel very badly for having dragged Nicole into all of this."

"Good." Chase had a plan, having remembered that Fritz had an important weakness—his car, a custom-made black Cadillac with gold grillwork. Fritz loved that car. It was his pride and joy. Chase had already noticed that the car was parked just down the street, out of sight of the house's windows, but where it could be seen from the sagging front porch. "Then go back in there and tell Fritz that his car has been stolen."

Leo swallowed nervously. His shining moment had come; his chance to right some of the wrongs he'd done. "I'll do it." He cleared his throat so that the next time he spoke he sounded less like a soprano. "I'll do it. Then what?"

"Then just stand back and stay out of the way."

Leo nodded, took a deep breath, ran his hand over his crew cut and then resolutely made his way back inside the house.

"So what's a nice girl like you doing in a place like this?" Fritz was asking Nicole.

"I've been asking myself that same question several times over the past few minutes," Nicole muttered. "I just came for some tea."

"Bad time to drop in for a visit," Fritz commented.

"Obviously so. I don't suppose you'd be inclined to let me go..."

Fritz shook his head.

Nicole sighed. "I didn't think so."

Nicole was making serious inroads on loosening the rope around her wrists when she heard Leo return. Time was running out.

"Your car's been stolen, Fritz!" Leo announced.

"*WHAT!*" Reacting instinctively, Fritz raced to the front door to look outside and see whether or not his precious car really was missing. Chase was ready for him as seconds later Fritz discovered that not only was his car gone, so was his gun—having been knocked out of his grasp by Chase. Shoving Fritz up against the peeling siding, Chase held the suspect still.

"You're breaking my arm!" Fritz wailed.

"You're lucky I don't break your neck," Chase growled before Chief Straud hurriedly took over.

Chase let the chief and the other officers read Fritz his rights. He had to get inside and make sure Nicole was all right.

Seeing him, Nicole smiled unsteadily. "It sure took you long enough, Detective," she murmured.

He rushed toward her, dropping down to his knees in order to hug her. It took him a second or two to realize that Nicole had her arms around his neck and was hugging him as fiercely as he was hugging her.

He leaned away to look at her. "How did you get loose?"

"I have a few hidden talents."

"Are you okay?" he asked, searching her face not only with tender fingers but with anxious eyes.

"I'm fine," she reassured him. "I wouldn't mind having my ankles untied however."

Chase leaned down and did that in no time at all.

Now she was free to stand up for their embrace. He slid his fingers through her hair, holding her head against his shoulder as if wanting to absorb her into his very being. Closing his eyes, he rocked her in his arms. "Don't ever do that to me again," he fiercely whispered, unknowingly using the very same words she'd used on him.

"What did I do?" she whispered back with a hint of a smile.

"You made me fall in love with you." The words were out before Chase could stop them.

Leaning away so that she could see his face, Nicole discovered that he looked almost as stunned as she felt. "You're upset," she excused him. "You're saying things you don't mean."

"Would you stop telling me what I mean? Trust me, I know what I'm talking about. I love you. I love your spirit and your honesty, your passion and your enthusiasm, not to mention your great legs," he added with an attempt at humor intended to diminish the tension still gripping him. "I've loved you for some time now. And now I know what you must have gone through—what it feels like to have someone you love in jeopardy. It's made me see things differently. I'll try not to take as many chances as I may have taken in the past. But I'm still a cop, Nicole. Think you can cope with that?"

Wondering if she'd live to see him again had forced Nicole to come to grips with her fears. Life and death situations had a way of boiling things down to their simplest elements. The end result was that Nicole had decided she wasn't going to let her fear of what might happen in the future prevent her from enjoying the here and now—*her* here and now—with Chase.

Life wasn't open-ended. It could cease at any moment, for her as well as for him. It seemed pointless to keep agonizing over the fact. It was time to start living and stop worrying about dying. "I'll cope," she stated firmly. "As long as you promise that you won't be quite as reckless as you've been in the past."

"I promise. But you've got to promise to be careful, as well," he told her.

"I do."

"I like the sound of that," he murmured, kissing her. "I'd like to hear you say it again—when you're dressed in a wedding gown and standing at the front of a church filled with people, saying 'I do' in front of everyone."

"Depends on who the groom is," she said, her heart filled with joyous anticipation.

"Me. What do you say?" He gently combed his fingers through her hair. "Do you want to take this undercover cop, for better, for worse, for richer, for poorer, in sickness and in health, to love and to cherish?"

"I do!"

Chase incorporated her laughter into their kiss as he promised her everything she'd ever wanted. It didn't matter that the room was filled with police officers or that Eddie was still tied up with a handkerchief in his mouth. When Eddie stamped his shackled feet on the floor to get some attention, the pounding matched the pounding of Nicole's heart as she pledged her love to the man who loved flirting with trouble.

"So Bruce Query, our illustrious board member's nephew, was the one facilitating things in the library." Nicole shook her head. She and Chase were cuddled together in her sleigh bed, enjoying the gift of being together. They'd already made love twice. "Querulous Query won't be amused. Do you know what's going to happen to Leo?"

"He'll probably get a suspended sentence and a hefty number of hours of community work. I recommended he do his community work at the library."

"That was sweet of you," she said.

"I'm a sweet guy," Chase mockingly replied.

"I know," she said quite seriously. She brushed her lips directly over his heartbeat. "That's one of the reasons why I love you."

"Why didn't you tell me earlier that you loved me?" he asked her.

"I was waiting for you to say it."

"Ever think that maybe I was waiting for you?" he countered.

"Ladies first, hmm?"

"In all things," he murmured wickedly, referring to the pleasure they'd just shared.

"There's something you should know about me," Nicole replied, sliding her hand down his chest and past his navel to caress him with seductive artistry. "I'm not always a lady."

"I know." His smile reflected his masculine pleasure. "That's one of the reasons why I love you so much." His kiss was filled with inexpressible satisfaction. "There's something you should know about me, too. It's a sign of how much I love and trust you that I'm willing to share this with you. Only three people on the face of this earth know this..." His voice trailed off meaningfully.

"What is it?" Nicole asked.

"My real name isn't Chase. It's a nickname my mom gave me when I was a kid, because she had to chase after me all the time. The name on my birth certificate is...Alvin. I hope this knowledge doesn't change the way you feel about marrying me..." he said with heroic stoicism.

"Well, Alvin Chase Ellis, the answer is still yes. I want to marry you. You're not getting away from me that easily."

"I'm not getting away from you at all," Chase murmured. "Not now. Not ever!" He sealed that heartfelt vow with a kiss.

* * * * *

⊘ SILHOUETTE®
Desire

What makes a Silhouette Desire?

It's ...

**SENSUOUS
SASSY
SPARKLING
SCINTILLATING
AND SIMPLY**

SPECTACULAR!

OFFICIAL RULES • MILLION DOLLAR BIG WIN SWEEPSTAKES
NO PURCHASE OR OBLIGATION NECESSARY TO ENTER

To enter, follow the directions published. If the Big Win Game Card is missing, hand-print your name and address on a 3″ ×5″ card and mail to either: Silhouette Big Win, 3010 Walden Ave., P.O. Box 1867, Buffalo, NY 14269-1867, or Silhouette Big Win, P.O. Box 609, Fort Erie, Ontario L2A 5X3, and we will assign your Sweepstakes numbers (Limit: one entry per envelope). For eligibility, entries must be received no later than March 31, 1994 and be sent via 1st-class mail. No liability is assumed for printing errors or lost, late or misdirected entries.

To determine winners, the sweepstakes numbers on submitted entries will be compared against a list of randomly preselected prizewinning numbers. In the event all prizes are not claimed via the return of prizewinning numbers, random drawings will be held from among all other entries received to award unclaimed prizes.

Prizewinners will be determined no later than May 30, 1994. Selection of winning numbers and random drawings are under the supervision of D.L. Blair, Inc., an independent judging organization whose decisions are final. One prize to a family or organization. No substitution will be made for any prize, except as offered. Taxes and duties on all prizes are the sole responsibility of winners. Winners will be notified by mail. Chances of winning are determined by the number of entries distributed and received.

Sweepstakes open to persons 18 years of age or older, except employees and immediate family members of Torstar Corporation, D.L. Blair, Inc., their affiliates, subsidiaries and all other agencies, entities and persons connected with the use, marketing or conduct of this Sweepstakes. All applicable laws and regulations apply. Sweepstakes offer void wherever prohibited by law. Any litigation within the province of Quebec respecting the conduct and awarding of a prize in this Sweepstakes must be submitted to the Régies des Loteries et Courses du Quebec. In order to win a prize, residents of Canada will be required to correctly answer a time-limited arithmetical skill-testing question. Values of all prizes are in U.S. currency.

Winners of major prizes will be obligated to sign and return an affidavit of eligibility and release of liability within 30 days of notification. In the event of non-compliance within this time period, prize may be awarded to an alternate winner. Any prize or prize notification returned as undeliverable will result in the awarding of the prize to an alternate winner. By acceptance of their prize, winners consent to use of their names, photographs or other likenesses for purposes of advertising, trade and promotion on behalf of Torstar Corporation without further compensation, unless prohibited by law.

This Sweepstakes is presented by Torstar Corporation, its subsidiaries and affiliates in conjunction with book, merchandise and/or product offerings. Prizes are as follows: Grand Prize—$1,000,000 (payable at $33,333.33 a year for 30 years). First through Sixth Prizes may be presented in different creative executions, each with the following approximate values: First Prize—$35,000; Second Prize—$10,000; 2 Third Prizes—$5,000 each; 5 Fourth Prizes—$1,000 each; 10 Fifth Prizes—$250 each; 1,000 Sixth Prizes—$100 each. Prizewinners will have the opportunity of selecting any prize offered for that level. A travel-prize option if offered and selected by winner, must be completed within 12 months of selection and is subject to hotel and flight accommodations availability. Torstar Corporation may present this sweepstakes utilizing names other than Million Dollar Sweepstakes. For a current list of all prize options offered within prize levels and all names the Sweepstakes may utilize, send a self-addressed stamped envelope (WA residents need not affix return postage) to: Million Dollar Sweepstakes Prize Options/Names, P.O. Box 7410, Blair, NE 68009.

For a list of prizewinners (available after July 31, 1994) send a separate, stamped self-addressed envelope to: Million Dollar Sweepstakes Winners, P.O. Box 4728, Blair NE 68009.

BWS792

SILHOUETTE Desire 10TH Anniversary

Celebrate with a FREE classic collection of romance!

In honor of its 10th anniversary, Silhouette Desire has a gift for you! A limited edition, hardcover anthology of three early Silhouette Desire titles, written by three of your favorite authors:

DIANA PALMER—*September Morning*
JENNIFER GREENE—*Body and Soul*
LASS SMALL—*To Meet Again*

This unique collection will not be available in retail stores and is only available through this exclusive offer.

Send your name, address and zip or postal code, along with six proof-of-purchase coupons from any Silhouette Desire published in June, July or August, plus $2.75 for postage and handling (check or money order—please do not send cash) payable to Silhouette Books, to:

In the U.S.	**In Canada**
Desire 10th Anniversary	Desire 10th Anniversary
Silhouette Books	Silhouette Books
3010 Walden Avenue	P.O. Box 609
P.O. Box 9057	Fort Erie, Ontario
Buffalo, NY 14269-9057	L2A 5X3

(Please allow 4-6 weeks for delivery. Hurry! Quantities are limited. Offer expires September 30, 1992.)   SDANPOP-R

SILHOUETTE DESIRE
10TH ANNIVERSARY
proof-of-purchase